samurai girl The Book of the Shadow

POCKET BOOKS
First published in Great Britain in 2004 by Pocket Books,
an imprint of Simon & Schuster UK Ltd
A Viacom Company
Africa House, 64-78 Kingsway, London WC2B 6AH

Originally published in 2003 by Simon Pulse an imprint
of Simon & Schuster Children's Division. New York

 Produced by 17th Street Productions, Inc.
A division of Daniel Weiss Associates, Inc.
33 West 17th Street, New York, NY 10011

A CIP catalogue record for this book is
available from the British Library

ISBN 07434 78363

1 3 5 7 9 10 8 6 4 2

Printed and bound in Great Britain by Cox & Wyman, Reading, Berkshire

The Asahi Shimbun

August 3, 2003

Heaven Help Her

Heaven Kogo, the adopted daughter of business mogul Konishi Kogo, was reported missing seven weeks ago after a violent incident during her wedding at Los Angeles' Beverly Wilshire hotel. Details of the incident are still unclear, but it appears that some type of attack was made. Several witnesses at the scene report that a ninja dropped through the ballroom skylight, although the Beverly Wilshire management was unwilling to comment on any damages sustained to their property. The attacker's identity and motive are still unknown, but the attack left Kogo's son, Ohiko, dead and countless guests and family members with minor injuries. It appears that the Kogo daughter escaped of her own volition, perhaps fearing for her life.

On Tuesday reports surfaced that Konishi Kogo has been attacked once more, this time in a Los Angeles restaurant, and has sustained serious injuries that have left him comatose. Mieko Kogo, Konishi's wife and Heaven's adoptive mother, refused to comment on her husband's health or her daughter's whereabouts, but several inside sources confirm both that Konishi remains comatose and that Heaven remains missing. Mieko Kogo is rumoured to be returning with her husband to Japan this week. It is unclear whether Konishi's serious condition may be enough to lure his runaway daughter out of hiding . . .

1

"Surprise," a voice said. The voice was dark, sinister, even smoky. I tensed up, searching the smooth green lawns of Hollywood in surprise. I could feel my heart clench and then *crack!* Suddenly I felt a sharp blow to my head, and pain exploded through my senses. I closed my eyes as my vision was flooded with white. I groped around for a moment, struggling in vain to get myself into a ready, defensive position.

Again. The word kept repeating in my brain – it was all I could think. *They've found me again. It's not over. It's me they want.* But there was no time for thinking now. Only for surviving.

My vision probably returned within seconds, but it felt like an eternity. Before me stood a huge Asian man, perhaps twice my size, with pulpy lips and an old beat-up black coat. He lunged at me again. The bright, sunny neighbourhood that surrounded Hiro's house suddenly seemed like a terrifying place. I guess *everywhere* seems terrifying when there's somebody determined to kill you.

"Heaven!" Hiro shouted, and I struggled to look at him. Someone else was there, too, beyond the guy who had just hit me. Somebody was also beating on Hiro. *Don't hurt him,* I thought frantically. It was one thing for me to be hurt in an attack – I was the one they were after. But not Hiro. *Oh God,* I thought as I tried to get into a ready position, *don't let me be responsible for him getting hurt.* Hiro and I were just returning from the airport, where we'd watched my comatose father get loaded onto a plane bound for Tokyo. I had thought – hoped, maybe – that it was my father these guys were after. Not me. *How did they find me here?* My mind was racing. *What do they want from me? When will this end?*

When the thug was inches away, I managed to whip my hand up and strike his shoulder with the back of my palm. He jumped back in pain, yelping, extreme surprise gleaming in his eyes. *That's right, baka,* I thought, relishing his high-pitched girlie yelp. *This little Japanese heiress can fight.*

He charged again. This time I was crouched down, ready for him. He ran into me like a thousand-pound sack of rice – he was fighting me more like a boxer than a samurai. I flailed around for a moment. He was so much stronger than I was. But *I* was smarter.

"Oof," I grunted, managing to wrestle myself free. I

4

glared at the thug's pulpy face. Hideous. Whoever was after me, he or she had a knack for finding the ugliest thugs in the universe. Then I looked down. *Oh, crap.* He was holding a knife. On instinct, I quickly grabbed for his throat in the "to hold down a pillow" move Hiro had taught me just days ago. Thank God we had just started learning how to disarm your opponent. I had to move quickly before he had a chance to do any damage. I heard my breath go in and out, as if I were wearing a scuba mask. Time seemed to slow down. My heart pounded in my chest.

I jumped forward, squeezing his throat and kicking his stomach. *"Oof!"* He recoiled in pain again, the knife flopping uselessly at his side. I began to feel dizzy, like I was going to fall over. My temples ached. I couldn't see Hiro anywhere.

Focus, Heaven, I screamed to myself. *For crying out loud, don't get all wimpy now.*

Suddenly I couldn't see anything; I didn't know where the guy had gone. I bent down to my knees, groping above to see if he was near. I struggled to remember Hiro's lessons about awareness, about trying to harness all of your senses to anticipate what would come next in the battle. As I crouched, I regained some of my vision and watched as the thug still grasped at his throat, struggling to breathe.

And then, out of the corner of my eye, I saw a miracle happen. Like divine intervention, a police car came slowly rolling around the corner. I don't think the driver saw the guy I was fighting, but the guy *definitely* saw the car. He freaked out and started running. I swivelled my head to find Hiro and saw that he didn't have any scratches. *I guess I should have known he'd be all right,* I thought. *Hiro kicks way more ass than I do.* The guy who'd jumped him had a bloody nose; when he saw the police, he bolted, too. Meanwhile the police, totally oblivious to what had just happened, turned onto another main street a few blocks down. Two pairs of shoes made empty echoes on the street, slowly dissolving into silence.

I could still feel each breath tearing through me. In and out. In and out. I could feel my body returning to normal as the adrenaline ebbed away.

Another attack. I'd survived another one.

"Oh my God," I murmured as I sat down on the curb, still gasping for breath.

"Are you all right?" Hiro rushed over to my side. My faithful protector. "Where did he hit you?"

"My head," I said, dazed. "Oh, Hiro, I'm so sorry . . ." I put my hand up to feel the wound. When I brought it back to my side, it was covered in blood. *Yuck.* I'd seen *way* too much blood in the past few weeks.

"Heaven, oh my—" Hiro started to say. He came closer and closer to me, looking at my head. Suddenly the whole world was spinning. It was like looking at kaleidoscope Hiro. The granola I'd had for breakfast that morning churned in my stomach.

"Heaven, your head," Hiro said, now right in front of me, his face next to mine.

Yes, I thought stupidly. *My head.* All I could focus on was my head, actually, because the rest of the world was completely spinning away. "Ugh," I whispered, and closed my eyes to steady the world. But after that, everything disappeared, even the pain.

I fell into a warm, comforting blackness.

2

I was back at the airport. Actually, this airport looked airy and much cleaner than LAX – more like Tokyo's Narita Airport. I looked down and realised I was wearing my wedding outfit again. Why? It felt incredibly constricting. The first thought I had was, *Oh my God, these last two months have been a dream. I'm actually going to marry Teddy*. It seemed like the worst thing in the world. But then I realised something.

My wedding kimono wasn't as it had been on my wedding day. Instead I was covered from head to toe in dried blood. Even my fingernails, my elbows, and my ankles were caked in it. I looked like something out of a Stephen King novel, like Carrie – the girl who was totally covered in blood at her prom.

For some reason, though, I didn't feel upset. I felt totally calm, like some kind of Zen master. I was on a higher plane – no pun intended. Outside the windows, I could see one lonely plane on the runway. It had Japan's red rising sun on its wing.

Looking to the right, I spotted a massive procession walking towards the plane. People marched slowly, carrying huge signs that bore photos of my father. My heart surged at the sight of him. The photograph was amazing: he looked powerful and self-satisfied, yet humble and intelligent. And on top of it all, a little scary. Just like in real life. I knew I'd seen the photograph somewhere – then I remembered where. It had been on the back of the annual report for Kogo Industries.

Behind them, a few large men slowly carried a coffin towards the plane. They were the kinds of guys my father would hold informal dinners with sometimes – big, greasy-looking men with expensive suits and weird, curly hair. I couldn't tell you their names. They were all wearing the exact same suit. They carried the coffin steadily without breaking stride – like robots.

I was watching my father's funeral.

I felt my stomach drop. My father had *died?* Why hadn't anyone told me?

Suddenly Hiro was standing next to me. He just sort of appeared, like a vapour. "Hello, Heaven," he said, and his voice was weirdly monotone.

"Hiro," I cried. "Thank God you're here! What's *happening*? When did my father die?"

"I'm sorry about your father's death," Hiro said, still in the same mechanical tone, staring straight ahead. "But it was a business decision. It could not have been helped."

"What do you mean?" I said, holding out my hands. There was something horribly familiar about that explanation. I looked down and realised that my hands were slathered in blood as well. Dried blood. It had caked and was a flaky brown.

"Did *I* kill him?" I asked with horror. Suddenly I completely believed that I had. I couldn't remember doing it, but I knew it was true – completely, horribly true. Tears sprang to my cheeks. Hiro grabbed my hand and squeezed it hard.

"I know," he said. "This must be terrible for you."

"It's all so terrible! Everything!" *Why did I kill him?* I was unable to control my tears. They poured down my face, leaving clean, wet trails through the dried blood. I wiped my face with my hand. But then Hiro leaned down and looked me in the eyes. He looked so beautiful. I thought how perfect his face was. He had a perfect mouth. And his expression – a look that seemed filled with desire, longing, love, pity, kindness, all at once – made my heart start beating faster.

And then something wonderful happened. Even in my dream, I could feel my whole body flood with happiness, like nothing I had ever felt before.

Hiro bent over and kissed me.

The kiss seemed to last forever. I leaned into him, running my hands through his hair. He grabbed me and pulled me closer to him. I could feel the strength and power of his body pressed up against mine. He felt so warm, like a blanket I wanted to curl up in. I didn't know what to do with this kind of desire – where do you go next? It was like I couldn't get close enough to him. I wanted to undress him and feel his whole body. I had never felt this way before; it was weird and wonderful all at the same time.

After what seemed like an eternity, we pulled apart. I kept

my eyes closed. I felt Hiro drop my hand. When I opened my eyes, Ohiko was standing at my side.

"Ohiko!" I breathed. "I – I thought I'd never see you again!"

My brother put his finger to my lips, pulled me close to him, and gave me a gigantic hug. He said nothing.

Then I remembered what my father had said right before he was wounded. *Ohiko was working for an enemy family. He was at the wedding as part of the attack, not to save you.* I pulled back from Ohiko and stared long and hard. Ohiko looked so kind, so gentle and innocent. How could what my father said have been true? "Why did you do it?" I asked.

"I didn't," Ohiko said. He shook his head over and over again. I knew that he was telling the truth. My father was the one who was wrong. I tried to speak but could not. It felt like my mouth was filled with gum. Then Ohiko began to call my name. "Heaven," he said. It seemed that he was becoming translucent. The funeral behind him had vanished. I suddenly felt terrible; I had missed the plane's takeoff.

"Heaven," he called softly. "Heaven."

I tried, but I couldn't manage to answer him.

"Heaven." Ohiko's calls were stronger now. Suddenly everything went white. I struggled to open my eyes but couldn't. "Heaven," boomed the voice again. Finally, with great effort, I managed to wrench my eyes open.

A shadowy figure stood above me, staring down. I couldn't quite focus on it. "Heaven," it said again.

"But you're dead," I said dreamily, not quite sure what was happening to me.

11

"What?"

I blinked. Now I could just make out Hiro standing above me, not my brother. "Are you okay?" he asked, his voice warm with concern.

"I just saw Ohiko," I babbled. Then I started to cry. My brother wasn't real. He had just been a dream. It was Hiro who was calling me, not my brother. I turned my head to the pillow and squeezed my eyes tightly together, trying not to completely lose it. I had heard that when those who have died appeared to you in a dream, it meant they were trying to speak to you. To tell you that everything was okay. But I didn't know whether to believe that. And why was my father dead? And my body covered in blood? What did that mean? "It's so terrible," I cried.

Hiro patted my shoulder. "I know, Heaven," he said, but my body continued to heave. "You've had a terrible day. I know this must be hard for you, having to read about your father's condition in the newspaper. Seeing your father in such a weakened state, to watch him fly off and not be able to do anything to help him . . . but you have to keep in mind, the paper said his condition is stable. He'll be all right. Right now we have to concentrate on protecting you."

I sobbed deeply into the pillow. Hiro was right. I remembered how my father had looked on his stretcher earlier today. Millions of tubes had sprouted from his body. I could barely see his face, but I knew in my gut that it was my father. My heart had recognised him even if my eyes couldn't. His silvery, efficient haircut, his tall, lean frame, the sharp shape of his nose. His face had looked pale and slack, and he'd been covered

12

by a white blanket almost up to his chin. A terrible lump had rushed up in the back of my throat; I'd felt almost nauseous. I had never seen my father hurt before. I'd never even seen him with a cold. To me, Konishi was invincible: tall, strong, even a little scary when crossed. It was hard to believe that my father had become this pale, wan creature. But I knew it was real. I had been there when he was wounded.

I had also seen my adoptive mother, Mieko. She'd worn a white jacket and hood, white pants, white shoes – white everything. My father loved it when she dressed all in white. It was just like Mieko to dress to please him, even when he was far too injured to care. I'd had a funny feeling as I watched her walk to the plane – I felt almost hurt that she'd never tried to contact me. Which was unfair, really. It had never occurred to me that Mieko was still in Los Angeles – I'd thought only of Konishi. The sight of her had reminded me that I had an adoptive mother, too, at least legally. Mieko had never been much of a real mother to me. Even now – was she trying to look for me? If she never saw me again, would she care?

I sniffled and rolled over. Hiro stared at me, but I couldn't quite look him in the eye.

"Are you okay?" he asked. "How's your head?"

"It hurts," I said. Those thugs. The knives. That sweaty body. *It's happening again.* My head throbbed as I tried to sit up. "What—?" I started.

Hiro shushed me. "Lie back down," he said, gently pushing me back onto the pillow. "You took a bad blow to your forehead, but I don't think you have a concussion. I think it was just a bad bump. I think you passed out more from shock."

"Those guys . . . ," I said hoarsely. They were definitely after me. It wasn't over yet. *Will it ever be over?*

"Shhh," Hiro said. He spoke in a very soft, calm voice. "Basically, Heaven, whoever is after you is still after you. And they've tracked you down to this neighbourhood. Thank God the police came when they did."

"I don't want to think about it," I muttered. Someone still wanted me. Some strange, phantom person – and they wanted *me,* not my father. I remembered the eyes of the ninja who'd attacked at my wedding – I had known even then that it was *me* he was after, even as I'd watched him slay my brother. A shiver ran down my spine. I wanted to go back to sleep. I wanted to sleep forever.

But then I realised something else. The thought made my stomach do flips, and I clutched the comforter to steady myself. The attackers had approached us just blocks from Hiro's house. Whoever these people were, they'd tracked me down to *this neighbourhood.* Which meant that their next stop would be Hiro's house itself.

Hiro was nothing to them. It was me they wanted. I thought of all the different movies I'd seen where criminals tried to get information out of an innocent man. I pictured Hiro tied to a chair in a dark basement, being beaten by thugs. I pictured him being burned with cigarettes or taunted with knives. They could kill him, beat him, torture him to get information on me. By staying with Hiro, I was endangering his life. And not in a "might happen someday" way – in a very real, very possible way. I didn't know how I could live with myself if anything ever happened to Hiro. He had given me everything – and he could have everything taken away, just for being kind to me.

I have to move, I thought miserably. *Find somewhere else to live.* The thought was as scary and terrible to me as someone else thinking, *I have to saw off my right arm.* I wasn't ready. Hiro was my anchor – he was the only person I could count on in L.A., and I couldn't give him up. Moving somewhere else and dealing with life on my own here, where there were killers out looking everywhere for me, seemed like a big, black cloud that could easily swallow me up. But I had to face it.

"Hiro, I think I should find somewhere else to live," I said.

Hiro's eyes widened. He sighed and shook his head, running his fingers through his dark hair. "I thought of that," he said quietly. "They've definitely tracked you to this neighbourhood. It's only a matter of time. I don't know what makes me more nervous, Heaven – the thought of you here, staying in this house when they're getting this close, or the thought of sending you out on your own." He looked at me. "Not that you're not strong enough to handle it. I'm sure you are. But I guess I feel that as long as you're living under my roof, I can protect you."

"Maybe no one can protect me." The words just kind of tumbled out of my mouth, but once they were out there, I realised how true they were.

Hiro's face turned grave. "*You* can protect you." He put his hand on my shoulder. "Remember that, Heaven." He stood up and walked into the kitchen. "I'm going to make some calls to see if I can find you a place to stay temporarily," he said. "Maybe Karen can help us out. She's got a pretty big place and I'm sure she wouldn't mind. Plus she lives in a different neigh-bourhood – Echo Park – which isn't far from here. You'll be safe for a while, anyway."

I nodded, trying to suppress a sigh. I knew Karen. She taught at the dojo. She'd acted a little weird towards me in the past – whenever Hiro was mentioned, she seemed to get a lit-tle competitive or angry. Maybe she was just a quirky sort of personality. Hiro went on: "I'm also going to check into some more permanent arrangements. We need to find somebody who's trustworthy and won't ask questions. I know a couple of people who might fit the bill. And I think from now on, you're going to have to disguise yourself when you go out. Wear sun-glasses and a hood or something to that effect. We know they're looking for you."

They. I shivered but didn't say anything. I just wished I knew who *they* were.

I slumped back on the couch, not sure what to do with myself. I had really set this whole thing in motion. I was really going to leave Hiro's place. I'd grown up in the same house all my life. The biggest adjustment I'd ever really had to face before a couple of months ago, when my life totally fell apart, was when our old chef Yotoyo quit and we hired a new one, Yoko, who put fish in everything, including the dessert. Also, I knew that moving would mean spending a lot less time with Hiro. He was my only real friend here. Who else did I know?

After all we'd been through the past two months, I felt like we really understood and cared for each other. Hiro was beginning to see how eager I was to become a samurai in the truest sense. In the fight with the ninja who had wounded my father, I had proved that I did not fear my own death but could face it with courage. Ever since then, Hiro had been treating me with a newfound respect.

I truly enjoyed being around him. I truly enjoyed what he was teaching me.

And, uh, oh, yeah – I was really starting to fall for him. In a totally nonbushido way of thinking, I wanted him to father my children. Or at least kiss me.

I remembered the good part of my dream. That kiss. *Damn.* It had felt so *real*. And so *good*. I blushed. The feeling of his kiss still burned on my mouth.

I rolled over on the couch and groaned. I'd never really thought out these feelings before, but there was no denying that I was into Hiro. I mean, who was I kidding? That dream, the kiss? That rushing, impatient feeling that swept over me? It was like my lust was leaking into my subconscious because I couldn't do anything about it in my waking life. Spending all this time with Hiro had not only made me feel secure, strong, purposeful, and protected, but it also made me feel completely besotted. With him.

After a while Hiro walked back into the room. He had a bowl of noodles in his hand. "Want some?" he asked, extending the bowl towards me. I shook my head. I was too keyed up to be hungry. He sat down in the chair opposite me and slowly began to eat the noodles. I found myself staring at his mouth. Those perfect lips. *Stop it, Heaven.*

"I just got off the phone with Karen," Hiro said. "She's on her way over here to pick you up."

"She's picking me up right *now*?" I said. I'd thought it would be another few hours! I wanted to stare at Hiro's poster of Mount Fuji and look longingly at his profile for just a little longer.

"She should be here in a couple of minutes," Hiro said. "But like I said, I don't think you should stay with Karen for long. She shouldn't get mixed up in this. I told her that you need another place to stay because you were mugged. It's close enough to the truth. She was really nice about it."

I sat up, not saying anything. I was too tense to speak.

Hiro went on. "If you want to look for a place on your own, that's fine, but like I said, I'll help you find a place. I know some people." Hiro paused, digging his chopsticks into the noodles. "If you want my advice, I definitely think you should look for a roommate situation, not for your own apartment. To get your own place, you have to have a job and up-front money for a security deposit, and they'll run a credit check on you."

"A credit check?" I asked.

"Yeah. You know . . . credit cards."

"I had a credit card," I said, drifting off. "My father paid the bill." I'd loved my credit card. My father had checked every item on the bill, but I was allowed to buy whatever clothes I wanted. Designer jeans, dresses I didn't need, thousand-dollar boots. I never had to worry about getting something I wanted. I just headed over to the mall and *swish, sign*, it was mine.

"Yeah, but they check into you, too. I don't think you want anyone checking into your background right now."

I sighed. Right. I didn't have even that much freedom now. Funny how someone trying to kill you totally limits your shopping options.

Hiro continued. "Also, Heaven, I've thought about it and I think you should look for a job. Since whoever it is you'll be staying with will probably demand something in the way of rent, you'll need to have some money coming in."

I began to wonder what Hiro would do if I hid under his bed and refused to come out. We'd talked about this before, but now I could see that I *really* needed a job. What would I be qualified to do? I gritted my teeth and thought about how when I was sixteen, I'd wanted to get a job down at Tower Records because some of my friends in school were working there, too. My father had been offended that I'd even brought it up. But if I had got that job, maybe I would feel a little more confident about finding a job *here*, in L.A., where not only was I completely unqualified but, now that I thought about it, I was also an illegal alien. It was doubtful that people would fall over themselves to hire me. Maybe I could sell my story to the tabloids. It was already plastered all over the regular papers; why not the *Enquirer*, too?

At least I was *qualified* to do that.

"But it will have to be a job that leaves time for training," Hiro said. "What about something like a coffee shop or a boutique?"

"Okay," I said. It came out as barely a whisper. I couldn't imagine holding down a job *and* doing our typical training day.

I had to stare at the wall to keep myself from crying. If only I could stay for even one more night, I was sure I'd feel better about the situation in the morning.

But that was out of the question. Hiro's safety was too important to me. He got up from his chair and stood next to me. "Promise me you'll start looking," he said. His face was close to mine. I could even smell the spiciness of the noodles he was eating.

"Of course," I said. *Kiss me,* I thought, totally inappropriately. "Are we – are we still going to train tomorrow?" I said, trying to pull myself together.

Hiro shook his head. "No training tomorrow. I don't want to risk it for a couple of days." Well, at least that would give me time to look for this job and new apartment.

Outside, a horn honked. "That's her," Hiro said. My heart sank.

"Gimme a minute," I blurted. I walked into Hiro's little bathroom and stared at myself in the mirror.

I looked positively horrific. My hair was going every which way, I had a nasty cut on my forehead, and my eyes looked puffy and bloodshot. I looked exhausted. God, I thought I'd been sitting there next to Hiro looking all sexy, fresh from battle, not a hair out of place. I guess that's only in the movies. I squeezed my eyes shut to block out the sight and tried to breathe.

Come on, Heaven. You can do this. Pull yourself together and go out there. You can deal with life. You have to. Think about what you've learned from training. Think about strength coming from within. With cowardice, you will die.

I left the bathroom. Hiro was standing at the door, already holding my bags. He must have seen my look of distress. I walked up to him and took the bags from his hands. "It'll be okay," he said firmly. "You know that, right?"

"I know," I said wearily. But I didn't know.

"I'll see you in a couple of days," Hiro said. There was an awkward pause. I tried to walk around him, but he stood in the way and I tripped over the carpet and fell into his back. "Oops," he said, catching me. I recovered my balance and blushed.

Hiro stepped to the side, still holding the door open. I smiled weakly and ducked my head and stepped forward. *Left, right, left, right, Heaven. Get it together.* "See ya," I said sheepishly. And then I turned to the outside, squinting in the sunlight, and walked shakily towards Karen's waiting car.

My husband's private plane is silent. I can hear his breath flowing in and out of his body. I stare out the window at the clouds. Clouds look the same wherever you go, whether you are in Japan or the United States or Antarctica. It does not matter.

I had imagined a different fate for us, when we returned to our country from this vulgar one. I had been to the United States a few times before and always cringed at the loudness and the flashing lights and the yelling. In Japan, yelling is considered extremely rude.

My husband could be called loud at times, but it is his actions that are loud, not his voice. He is loud when he is angry. Loud when someone has done something to anger him. And my precious son, Ohiko, angered him terribly. He would not hear Ohiko's pleas for his understanding. He merely sat with a rigid mouth. I did not say anything. I have found that it is best to practise the code of nakatta koto ni suru: pretend it did not happen. Out of sight, out of mind. It is the best way.

I just want to make him comfortable. In America, the doctors screamed over his head as he lay somewhere beyond us, in the clouds. I was on the phone with Aryoshi in Tokyo. Give me the best medical team you've got. Give me people he knows. For Konishi, they do anything.

He cannot tell me how he is feeling. American doctors told me nothing. He woke up once and sat up. His eyes bore a look of akuma, a devil. "Heaven," he cried. Then he lay back down. I was stunned. I asked the doctors what was happening to him. They would tell me nothing. Nothing.

I feel a twinge of guilt and fear and . . . excitement. Heaven's life is changing. And there is nothing he can do about it. He is not able to control anything now.

I see Mount Fuji ahead. It is covered in snow. I think of Yuki-Onna, the Lady of the Snow. In the folktale, a master and his apprentice are travelling through the snowy regions of Kyoto. They find a place to sleep in a ferryman's hut. But the apprentice does not sleep; he stays awake. He sees a strange woman come into the hut, standing above his master. She blows snowy ice into the master's face and kills him. She says to the apprentice, "If you tell anyone about this, the same thing will happen to you."

The next year the apprentice is returning home and meets a young woman in these same woods. She is beautiful; she says her name is Yuki. They marry; Yuki provides him with ten children. One night, while Yuki is sewing, sitting by the fire, the apprentice looks at her and says, "You remind me so much of this beautiful woman I saw when I was eighteen years old. She killed my master with her ice-cold breath. I'm sure she was a strange spirit, but tonight she resembles you." Yuki looked up at him with a terrible expression on her face. "You fool," she said. "It was I, Yuki-Onna, who came to you that night and silently killed your master! You promised you would keep the secret, though, didn't you? If it weren't for those children of yours sleeping in the next room, I'd kill you now." Instead she changed into a white mist, never to return again.

Some say she lives in the mountains. She is a silent killer. She is full of secrets.

I am entranced by this story.

"We should be reaching Tokyo shortly," Ichi, the pilot, says to me. I nod.

"Arigato," I say. My husband's heartbeat rolls out in waves.

Mieko

3

"Hey!" Karen called as I rushed down the sidewalk and threw my bags in the back of her little car. She looked utterly perfect, as usual, the bitch, in a sleeveless cowl-neck sweater and striped cords. I tried not to sigh. My T-shirt still had blood on the shoulder. *Blood*.

"How's it going? Are you all right?"

"Yeah," I lied. I was totally *not* all right. But no need to get Karen involved in all that. *After all,* I thought, *the attack could have been much worse.*

"Hiro said you got mugged," Karen said, looking me over with an expression that seemed halfway between concern and suspicion. Did she not believe Hiro? He'd said she was cool about it, but this wouldn't be the first time she'd acted weird to me when Hiro wasn't around.

"Yeah," I said with a big sigh, and looked out the window. "Thank you so much for taking me in. It was kind of traumatic. I'd rather not talk about it."

25

Karen was silent for a minute, and the car was so quiet, I could hear her breathing in and out. "I understand," she said finally, and I heard her putting the car into gear. "Let's get out of here. I rented some movies for us to watch."

I watched Hiro's house slowly fade into the distance as Karen pulled away. My heart sank, and all I could think was, *How can I possibly handle life without him?* Then I tried to tell myself I was being a big dork. It wasn't like I would never see Hiro again. And I would make it on my own, just like I had survived when I first ran away from my wedding. I had to calm down. I knew I liked to overdramatise: Sometimes I overreacted to things, thinking that my life was a part of a movie script. Cue the tears, cue the melodrama. Sometimes I expected to be accepting the Best Actress award for my brilliant performance as myself.

Karen maneuvered the car easily along the freeway. That old No Doubt song "Just a Girl" was playing on the radio. "Can I turn it up?" I asked, trying to snap myself out of my funk. "I love this song." In Tokyo, when this song would come on, Katie, my English tutor, and I would get up and dance like lunatics. We would thump and crash into things and drive the servants crazy. They all thought we were having seizures or something.

Maybe Katie and I weren't the best dancers.

"Sure," Karen said with a smile. "This is a great song."

I nodded. Karen was always very composed, very cool – except for this one time when we'd practised attacks and she'd started to act a little bit insane. I had this feeling she might be jealous of my living situation with Hiro. She seemed like a good person to stay with, though. She didn't ask many questions about the strange state of my life.

We pulled up to this cute little bungalow on this tucked-away street in a neighbourhood called Echo Park. "Echo Park is sort of an up-and-coming neighbourhood in L.A.," Karen explained. "It's got kind of an artist's feel to it, and the rents are cheaper than a lot of neighbourhoods. Hiro tells me you're looking for your own place. This wouldn't be a bad neighbourhood to look in. There's a lot going on here."

I nodded again. Karen's house was small but cute. There was a tiny garden out front with tulips and azalea bushes. The bungalow was painted tan with darker brown trim, and it seemed to be carefully tucked into the corner of a hill. Cosy. Before we even went inside, Karen stopped me and gave me a serious look. "I apologise in advance," she said. "My house is a little messier than it usually is. I've been a little distracted lately, and . . . well, hopefully it won't be a big deal."

"Believe me," I said. "It won't matter."

When we stepped inside, I didn't know what mess she was talking about. Karen's place was far cleaner than Hiro's. I couldn't believe how spotless and scrubbed everything looked. *Anal retentive much?* I thought, then immediately felt bad for having mean thoughts. After all, Karen was taking me in when no one else would. And her house was nice overall. Comfortable. It had a funky feel about it – new, cute furniture and paper lamps everywhere. She'd hung lots of stuff up on the walls – a conglomeration of flyers from the neighbourhood

27

clubs, strange postcards, weird artwork. Stacks of CDs adorned one wall. It was all very neat and organised but kind of had a more funky, upbeat feel than Hiro's place.

We stood there shivering a minute after from coming in from the unseasonably cold weather. "Do you have a warmer coat you can wear if this weather keeps up?" Karen said, studying me.

"I have a coat of Hiro's that I can wear," I said. "A windbreaker. I have it in my bag." I was glad I had that coat. I remembered it smelled like Hiro.

"Oh, right," Karen said, sort of distracted, as she walked into the kitchen and took off her jacket. Was I imagining things, or was there just a tiny hint of coldness in her voice? I frowned, watching Karen's back as she walked over to the phone and picked it up. "I'm just going to check my voice mail," she called casually. Was it just that I was trying to create drama with Karen? Or was she seriously jealous of me and Hiro?

I walked back into the living room. The thought of Hiro brought me back to our awkward goodbye. I'd *slammed* into him! *Why* had that goodbye been so awkward? Was there something Hiro had wanted to say? My mind spun. I thought about his lips, his eyelashes. His wonderful smooth skin. *Maybe Karen has reason to be jealous of me.*

I let out a long, dreamy, loud sigh.

"Are you feeling okay?" Karen said from the other room. "Something wrong?"

"I'm fine," I said. I guess I'd sighed too loudly. "Just tired."

"Listen, maybe you're just stressed out. I mean, you've

been through a lot today. Being mugged isn't fun. I got mugged in San Francisco once, and I was freaked out for a week." She came out of the kitchen and gave me a curious look. "You reported it to the police, right?" she asked. "You should help them catch this jerk. Before he goes and mugs someone else."

I nodded. "Oh, we told the police. They, um, took my statement and everything."

Karen's smile returned. "Good. Hiro's neighbourhood can get pretty dicey, I hear."

"Uh-huh," I said, quickly remembering what Hiro had said: *Karen should stay out of this.* He and I had made an agreement that we'd try to keep what was happening with me – the attacks, my father, Teddy, ninjas, all of it – as quiet as possible. The more people who knew, the more people who might get hurt.

Karen went over to her couch and fluffed a couple of pillows. "How about we watch the movies I rented? We can lounge and relax."

"Okay," I said slowly. Watching movies actually sounded great. I hadn't been able to do this in ages. Karen's couch had the most comfortable cushions I'd ever sat on. Soon enough we had popped in *Sixteen Candles,* a movie I'd seen tons of times back in Tokyo with Katie. Laughter came easily. I began to feel a little bit safer. Before long I found my mind drifting. Suddenly my mind was filled with pictures of Hiro: I saw him in that same way he'd come to me in my dream, romantic, ideal. I imagined what it would feel like to just lean in and kiss him. I hugged myself and flexed my toes in and out, filled with a delicious but anxious sense of lust.

Was it me, or had he been looking at me like he wanted to say something else when I left? There was one time earlier this week when we'd been preparing dinner together and Hiro had turned to me and opened his mouth to say something. "What?" I'd asked. "There's—" he said, then stopped. "What?" I asked again. "What is it?" Hiro shook his head.

"Never mind," he said. "It's not a big deal." I hadn't really thought too much of it then – sometimes Hiro got lost in his own thoughts – but now I wondered. What had he been trying to tell me? My heart hammered. Would there be a day when Hiro would admit that he felt something for me? What if I said something to him first? No way. I was too afraid he would laugh at me or something. I might have grown braver in my martial arts skills, but as far as love was concerned, I was a complete rookie.

"Heaven?"

I jumped. "Huh?"

Karen laughed. "I've been talking to you for ten minutes now and you haven't said a word."

"Oh," I said. Really?

"You seem about a million miles away. You had the strangest look on your face just then," Karen said. "What's going on?"

I tried to snap myself out of it. What was I doing? I was in the home of a girl I didn't know very well, letting my imagination run away with me. I straightened up. Could I really open

30

up to Karen? How much did she really know about my life?

"Nothing, really," I said. "I'm just tired, that's all." I didn't know how much to explain. I felt that so much was swirling in my head and I needed to get it out, but maybe Karen wasn't the right person to talk to. She acted sort of strange whenever I brought up Hiro. I didn't totally trust her.

"Are you sure?" Karen said in a soft voice. "If you want to talk about anything . . ."

I sighed. The truth was, I *really* wanted to talk. Not just about Hiro – about everything. Being on my own. Finding an apartment. I so missed my long talks with Katie. Hiro could be a great listener, but there was just something about having a girlfriend to talk to. And Karen was being so nice about it . . . Maybe there was a way I could disguise who I was talking about? Maybe if I pretended I had a thing for someone else, Karen would stop acting weird.

"I'm just a little overwhelmed, that's all," I said. Once I started, the words just came flooding out of me. "I have to both get a job and find a new apartment in, like, less than a week. I've never had to do anything like this before. My dad in Tokyo was way overprotective. He wouldn't *allow* me to get a job. So what am I even qualified to do? How can I get a job and expect to train at the dojo as well? And how can I do all that *and* find a new apartment? How did you do it? How do you, like, you know, *live*? How do you make decisions for yourself? How do you deal with . . . everyday things? Honestly, I just want to hide under someone's bed for the rest of my life. But that's not an option . . ."

Once I started talking, it felt good to admit my fears to someone, even if I wasn't sure what to expect.

Karen smiled. "I admit it's hard at first. Like I said, I didn't grow up here but moved out to get a change of scenery. But let me tell you, it's the best thing in the world to be on your own. You learn a lot about yourself, and other people, and . . ." She trailed off. She stared at something random on the wall. It was like she was one of those battery-operated toys whose batteries had just run out.

"Um, hello?" I said tentatively.

Karen blinked. "Oh God, I'm sorry. I've been totally spacey lately. But really, Heaven, it's scary and great at the same time. You'll really appreciate the experience once you've been through it."

Great. I had to get *through* it first before I could *appreciate* it. What if I was dead before I got through it? The deeper meaning of what I was saying and not saying chilled me to the bone. Karen had no idea that there were thugs attacking me and other, invisible people who were after me. Those things worried me even more than striking out and making a life for myself. What if there was no one to defend me? Was I ready?

I threw myself back on the pillow.

"You have to take it one day at a time," Karen said in a dreamy voice.

That was actually true. If I got a job and an apartment, maybe I'd be hidden from these attacker guys. Maybe I could find *them* before they found *me*.

I took a deep breath. "There's something else, too," I said.

"What?" Karen said. My tone of voice must have caught her attention.

I closed my eyes and tried to pretend that my life really *was* a movie, and this was going to be my Academy Award–winning performance. "Promise you won't say anything to anyone," I said, opening them.

"Of course not. What is it?" Karen asked.

"Well, okay." I took another deep breath. "I've been in the United States for a month, but there's this boy I like back in Japan."

"Oh! Back in Japan?" Karen's eyes widened just a little. If I'd blinked, I would've missed it, but for a second there she definitely looked surprised.

"Yeah. And" – I let out a deep sigh – "I *really* like him. We've been good friends for a while. We spent a lot of time together, and he had been trying to tell me things, and I think he might have really been interested in me, but he never fully finished his thought."

Karen nodded slowly. "I see," she said.

"But there's a pretty good chance I'll see him again. Not anytime soon, I mean, because he's in *Japan*, but someday. Do you think . . . is there any way to figure out whether he's really interested? Maybe I should make the first move. Or try to make him jealous. Or something." I looked over at Karen, trying to look innocent and sincere while I repeated my words back to myself and tried to make sure there was no hint that I was really talking about Hiro.

Karen looked at me for a long time. After a few seconds my

heart began to pound about a million times a minute. I was sure that she had figured me out. I felt like there was a giant blinking sign on my head that said IT'S NOT A BOY FROM TOKYO – HEAVEN LOVES HIRO! But to my surprise, she finally smiled and nodded and said, "I don't give advice too much, but do you really want to know what I think?"

"Um, yes." It was so weird to talk about this. Even though I'd known for a while that I was into Hiro, I guess it had been floundering in the back of my head – not really poking to the surface. Saying the words out loud made it seem much more serious.

"Well, Heaven, if he really likes you, he'll let you know. There might not be anything more than that. But believe me, he'll let you know how he feels. That's the only way it's ever happened to me."

"Uh-huh," I said. Karen looked in the other direction. She looked like she'd suddenly got wrapped up in the beginning of *You've Got Mail*. Was there any way she could have figured out I was talking about Hiro? *No,* I told myself. *Stop being paranoid and just take her advice.* I had the feeling it was good advice. If I could just be myself, things with Hiro would fall into place. And honestly, I had a feeling they were heading in the right direction already.

Suddenly the phone rang. Karen shot up like the chair was on fire and ran to get it. "Hi, Hiro," she said after a couple of seconds. My stomach did a little flip. I sat up, expecting Karen to give the phone over to me, but she didn't. Instead she went farther into the kitchen, moving out of earshot. I could hear her say, "Yes . . . yes. Heaven is fine. Yeah . . . we were here all day. Nothing out of the ordinary happened." Then she went into her room and I could only hear bits and pieces of the conversation.

Something suddenly seemed fishy. Why was Karen going into her bedroom to talk to Hiro? Was she telling him something about me? A knot formed in my stomach. What if she was telling Hiro about the Japanese guy I'd told her about? Hiro would definitely ask questions or say it completely wasn't true . . . and then . . . oh my God . . . what if they figured out that I was actually talking about *Hiro*? What if they were having a big laughathon over Heaven and her stupid crush? *Like she has a shot!* I imagined Hiro saying. My cheeks burned. I sat up a little taller on the couch to hear Karen.

"That sounds terrible," I heard her say in a weirdly sweetened voice, very different than the unaffected tone she'd used with me and while she was at the dojo. Again I clenched my teeth. What *exactly* were these two saying about me?

I heard Karen giggle. "Oh, you!" she said lightly. Then, "Yeah . . . I know . . . me too. Definitely." She was speaking so softly that I didn't think she was saying anything about me. And if they weren't talking about me, what were they talking about?

Oh, no.

Oh, *no*.

What if . . . what if . . . they . . . what if . . . ?

I suddenly felt like someone had punched me in the stomach. I even doubled over, although that made me feel worse. I couldn't wait for Karen to hang up the phone. My mind rewound back to her dazed looks all day and her cryptic comment about *If a boy likes you, he'll let you know. That's the only way it's ever happened to me.*

What an idiot I'd been.

All day today we'd been spacing out over the same guy.

I put my head in my hands. Maybe it wasn't true. But when Karen finally strolled back into the living room, she wore a goofy smile on her face. "Hey," she said to me breezily.

"Was that Hiro?" I realised too late that my voice had come out like a bark.

"Yeah," Karen said. "I told him what we were up to today and, you know."

I saw her cheeks grow rosy.

"Karen . . . ," I said very slowly, feeling like a knife was being applied right between my shoulder blades, "is something going on between you and Hiro? Are you guys, like, more than friends?"

I pasted on the fakest-looking smile in human history. I think I looked like Krusty the Clown from *The Simpsons. Hey hey!* I felt like my true feelings for Hiro were scribbled all over my face with a gigantic Magic Marker. Surely Karen would look up and see.

But she just smiled. I guess when you're that happy, it's hard to be bothered by the total *misery* of those around you. "Well, I didn't want to say anything, because it kind of just started, and I know you're a friend of his. But yeah." She took my hand in hers, all girl-talk excitement. I briefly entertained the thought of squeezing her hand so hard, my knuckles would turn white. "Yeah, something's starting, I think. At least it's heading that way." She sat back down on the couch, becoming her cool, collected self again.

"That's great," I said limply. My stomach sank to my knees and my lip wobbled. I was sure all the colour had been sucked out of my face. I felt like a complete and total idiot, but I kept looking at her with this frozen grin. Inside, I was so far away from smiley. I had never in my life heard anything *less* great.

*I keep tossing and turning in bed. I can't get a good posi-
tion. I try to do some yoga pranayama breathing to calm myself
down, but I'm way too excited. I've had this experience only a
couple of other times. There was James, back in San Francisco,
who lived only a block away from me. We used to walk to school
together, six short streets, filing in. We would walk silently. Our
hands would brush together, dance. And then one day when we
were about to go inside, maybe a block away, up against a building, he kissed me. James was a year older. I had never kissed
anyone before. At first I didn't know what to do, but then somehow I did. Somehow my mouth and hands knew where to go. I
remember thinking,* Wow, I'm kissing someone. This is what it's
like. *With James, with kissing, it seemed to come naturally.*

*Kissing Hiro has come naturally, too. He has such a gor-
geous mouth. The first time we kissed was only days ago. He'd
been dancing around it and then we were in his office at the
dojo together, talking. I felt that way you feel when . . . I don't
know . . . you know someone likes you. And it felt so good. I
had been thinking about him for weeks, and then . . . finally . . .
it seemed that Hiro would go out of his way to be around me,
be near me, touch me. I remember reading a magazine article
on body language and how to tell if someone is interested. If
they're leaning towards you, working to get close, then that's
a big sign. Hiro was always leaning in.*

*When we first kissed, he stared at me intensely and took
my hands and lowered me down to my knees and leaned down
from his chair and his lips met mine. He didn't explain himself;
he just did it. That made it even sexier. He held my face and*

then pulled his hands through my hair and locked his fingers behind my head. And again, as with James, I knew exactly what to do. I closed my eyes. I let the sensations carry me away.

When it was over, I stared at him, not surprised, not shocked, just stared a confident stare. But I have to say I got a little scared afterwards. I'm a little scared now. This feeling seems so much bigger – better – than with James. Back then, we were kids. With Hiro, I think I could invest something . . . I feel like it could really go somewhere.

I am getting completely careless thinking about Hiro. I told Heaven about us; I wonder if I should have. I guess she would've found out soon enough. I wonder how Hiro will tell her. He seems so protective of her. And the truth is – really – I had been totally convinced that she felt something for him. *Just something about the way she looked at him, the way she seems uncomfortable, unhappy, whenever she's not with him. But now she gives me this new information about a guy she likes in Japan. Still – could she be making that up? Why would she? I guess her attachment to Hiro is understandable, considering her situation. And he's not even telling me half of what's going on now. But I'm burning to know. I know it's none of my business. But I'm still wildly curious.*

Karen

4

The next morning I rolled over and stared at a wall that I didn't recognise. I shot up in bed.

Where the hell was I?

Oh. Right. Karen's.

Karen, who's dating Hiro.

My stomach dropped down into my toes.

I could hear noises in the other room. Karen must already be up. *Karen, who's dating Hiro.* I stumbled into the kitchen to see her, fully dressed in dark jeans and a flowy top. Her bag containing her neatly folded cotton gi jacket, obi, and flowy cotton pants sat by the door. She was sitting at the table, having a cup of tea. I gritted my teeth: She looked perfect. She *always* looked perfect. And I looked . . . like I'd just stumbled out of bed.

"I see you're up," Karen said with a smile. "How are you feeling?"

"Okay." I immediately felt bad. I knew it was wrong to be

mad at Karen. It wasn't like she knew where my imagination had gone. It wasn't like she'd stolen Hiro out from under me in any place but my own head.

Actually, now that I'd slept on it, I wondered if maybe it was Hiro I should feel annoyed at. Why didn't he tell me what was going on? It was pretty hard to hide anything from me, what with me living in his apartment, working out at his dojo. So why had he gone out of his way not to tell me he was involved with Karen? I knew he had a right to privacy, but I hated feeling like he didn't trust me. That time earlier this week when he'd stopped and tried to tell me something – maybe that was it. But he'd stopped himself. Why? I felt even younger and dumber than I had yesterday.

"You going to be okay here on your own?" Karen asked, sipping her tea.

I shrugged. "I guess so." A little streak of nerves sang through my stomach. Today I had to do things. Real things. Things everyone else in America probably did without batting an eyelash, but which seemed impossible to me. Beyond impossible. *It's all right, Heaven,* I told myself. *One step at a time.*

"You going to look for a job?" Karen said, flipping quickly through the *L.A. Times*. "The best way would probably be to look through the help-wanted ads in the *Times,* here. Or in this Echo Park paper." She rifled through some mail until she found a thin-looking newspaper. "You might be able to find apartment listings in here, too – although you can stay here as long as you want, of course."

41

Right, I thought. *I'm sure you'd be thrilled to keep me around, sitting right between you and Hiro on the couch. Instead of you two making out, we can all play a big game of Uno.*

"Thanks," I muttered. I wouldn't be able to move out fast enough.

Karen checked her watch and shot up. "I'm going to be late if I sit around here any longer," she said, putting her cup in the sink.

"Do you eat breakfast?" I asked her.

"I pick up something at a juice bar near the dojo," Karen explained. "Usually a wheat grass shot and some bulgur wheat and tofu and scrambled eggs. But there's some multigrain cereal in the cupboard. And edamame, if you feel like a snack."

"Oh. Okay." I'd been hoping for some ridiculously sugary cereal. Or a doughnut. Maybe that was too much to dream of in L.A.

Karen grabbed her coat and keys. "You sure you'll be all right?" When I nodded, she opened the door. "All right, see you later!"

"Bye." I watched blankly as Karen disappeared through the front door. Then I sat down at the table with a glass of water. The house was so quiet now – it was really unsettling. I stared at the wall for a little while, feeling sorry for myself. *Stupid wall,* I thought. *Stupid wall gets to sit in the house all day, just holding up the roof and a couple of pictures. Stupid wall doesn't have to go out and find a job.* Then I squared my shoulders and rolled my neck around in a circle. What was *wrong* with me? Envying a wall? Why was I being such a baby? "What is your *problem*?" I said to myself out loud. "Get a grip, Heaven! People look for jobs every day!"

I remembered Karen's words last night. *You'll really appreciate the experience once you've been through it.*

A great experience. At least something like that would get my mind off Hiro and the people trying to kill me.

I squared my shoulders and picked up the paper. Quickly scanning it for any news of my father (nothing, thank God), I flipped to the Classifieds section. Amazingly, there were quite a few listings for the kind of "want fries with that?" jobs I would be qualified for right here in Echo Park. Most of the ads said to come down to the places to apply. There was even an ad for an artist's assistant in Los Feliz, one neighbourhood over. How fun would that be? I circled some of the ads I saw, then found some more in the Echo Park paper, ripped out the pages, and stuffed them into my coat pocket.

I realised then that my stomach was snarling. I walked over to Karen's cupboard and pulled out her box of no-sugar-added wheat-free granola. I shook it. The box weighed a ton. What did you put in wheat-free granola? Rocks? What I *really* wanted right now was a Krispy Kreme. I'd noticed there was a store full of them right down the street from Karen's house. I deserved a doughnut for getting out there and starting my new life, right? Of course I did.

Things were looking better already.

Unfortunately, that artist's assistant job I was talking about? Complete bust. There was a line of qualified college kids in front of me just dying for the job, so I didn't even hang around for it. Instead, I did what I think is called pounding the pavement. I must have gone to thousands of little shops, eateries, diners, coffeehouses, bakeries. I even asked if Krispy Kreme was hiring, but they weren't. Every place on my list kindly gave me an application to fill out, but I felt a little nervous writing down my name and address. Some ice-cream store manager asked me what my "social" was and I stared at him blankly. "Where you from?" he asked. "Japan," I said quietly. He shook his head. "No social security number, no job," he said. "We don't pay under the table here."

So, lesson number one: I had to find a job that "paid under the table." Whatever that meant. I had a feeling it wouldn't be easy.

One bagel place I walked into seemed willing to hire me, and the manager said he was cool with "paying under the table." It looked nice enough until I saw a huge, nasty rat scurrying into the back room. The back room that, presumably, I'd be working in. Well, *gross*. I might have fallen far from my servants and unlimited credit cards and personal chauffeur, but I wasn't quite ready to throw in the hat and live like a *Survivor* contestant just yet. No rats for me, thank you very much. I still had enough money for doughnuts and my pride.

Then I sat down at a coffee shop for an interview and was immediately weirded out by the gross manager's sudden eyebrow movements. "We've already hired someone," he said with a smarmy grin, flicking his left eyebrow skywards. "But you look so delicious, I could maybe hire you just for eye candy." I looked at him in surprise, and the guy just licked his lips as he looked me up and down. I suddenly felt dirty – this guy was at least twice my age. "No, thanks," I said, grabbing my application and stalking out the door. I'd changed my mind – *this* was my new low. I was ready to give up.

I crossed out all the places I had gone to. Of the fifteen or so places I'd circled, I was down to *one*.

The place was called Life Bytes. It was in a particularly dingy section of Chinatown. It took me forever to get there, and my feet felt sore and blistered. The place was a storefront building attached to a few others. A piece of plywood hung at the top, strangely painted in neon colours, but I couldn't exactly make out what it said. It was painted in big swirly letters, like graffiti. I only knew I was at the right place because of the number on the door.

The ad had said this place was a cybercafé. I remembered reading about cybercafés quite a few years back. I hadn't seen any others since I'd got to L.A, so I didn't know exactly what was in store for me.

I pushed open the door. The place was small, with a bunch of high-tech computers propped up against the far wall. The computers were all occupied by an impressive array of clients: dorky white guys, Asian hipsters, and a few kids young enough to make me check my watch and see if school was out (it was – I'd been wandering around for hours). On the other wall was a sleek silver bar with a shiny orange espresso machine. Two large coffee tureens burbled, one with an orange top, the other with chrome. Strange, trancelike techno pumped through the speakers. Everyone was tapping away furiously, pausing to talk on their tiny silver cell phones in Mandarin. I even overheard someone speaking Japanese. This place was so secluded and high-tech, I felt like a signal could be given and the whole place could be converted into a giant war room with computer consoles rising from the ground and a big TV screen dropping from the ceiling.

Suddenly a round, pale, overly eager face swam before me. "Hello!" it said. "Do you want to use the computers?"

"Um. I was . . . the job . . . ?" I couldn't get my thoughts out correctly. The guy was staring at me oddly. He had terribly cut hair – maybe he cut it himself – and wore a *Futurama* T-shirt. He was looking at me, in all honesty, as if he'd never seen a girl before. As if I was a new specimen for his jar.

"A job! The job in the paper!" the guy said happily. "Of course!" He thrust out his hand, and I shook it hesitantly. "I'm Farnsworth. So you're interested in employment?" He had a funny twitch about him and spoke with a hint of a lisp.

I wrung my hands together. "Well, I don't know." I looked around. "It doesn't seem like you need anybody." No one was in the line for coffee. No one even had coffee cups at their computer terminals. How did this place make money?

"Nonsense! Of course we do!" Farnsworth said, waving his hands. "I'm the manager. I posted the ad."

I looked at a little button on his shirt. "Actually, it says you're the assistant manager," I said.

Farnsworth blushed. "You're smart! See, we *do* need you! Well, it's true – a guy named Scott Shou owns the place, and he's the *official* manager, but he's never around, and he okayed me hiring someone. We need somebody to man the counter, do a little sweeping and mopping, you know. That kind of stuff."

I could tell some of the guys at the computers were listening. They'd taken their headphones off and were sort of staring past me, at the wall. They made me a little nervous. Especially the one who was speaking Japanese. Did he recognise me from the papers?

"Um, I don't know if I'm interested," I said, polite as I could be. The place kind of gave me the creeps. "But thank you—"

"The salary," Farnsworth interrupted me, "is twelve dollars an hour. Under the table."

I gasped. It was double almost every other place I'd been to.

Farnsworth looked at me with a serious face. "Is that too low? Fifteen an hour. How's that?"

"I . . . um, that sounds good," I murmured. Fifteen an hour, I'd be in an out-of-the-way location, and maybe I could even get some use out of the Internet. Maybe it wouldn't be so bad. The money was more than I'd imagined. I had to find a job somewhere. I couldn't imagine spending another day like I had today – humiliatingly trudging from place to place, admitting I had no experience, unable to give a phone number where I could be reached. Farnsworth seemed perfectly harmless. The other guys would be fine, as long as I kept my distance. If it was weird, I could get out.

I asked Farnsworth about hours and flexibility, and he seemed totally cool with working around my training time. I got the feeling I'd found a real gem here – they were paying me to make up my own schedule and not do much at all.

"I'll take it," I said, taking a deep breath.

"You will?" Farnsworth said, almost bursting at the seams. "That's great!" He stuck out his hand for me to shake. I put my hand into his delicately. His palm was a little sweaty now, as if he were nervous. He pumped my hand up and down. "Congratulations, and welcome aboard!" he said. I smiled weakly.

Farnsworth rushed over to a little hole behind the counter, which led to a back room. He emerged with a set of papers. "Some stuff for you to fill out." He winked at me. "Just so I can reach you if we need extra help, that kind of thing." I bit my lip and thought for a moment. Did I really want to give Karen's address or phone number?

"Do you mind if I don't fill these out right this minute?" I asked. "I'm sort of in transition right now as far as an address goes. Can I finish this when I find a new place?"

Farnsworth shrugged. "Sure, that's fine. I probably won't need to contact you right away, anyway."

"I'm in the process of finding a new place right now," I explained.

Farnsworth walked over to the three nerdy guys at the computers. "Heaven," he said. "I want to introduce you to my homeys over here. There's Rom, Shigeto, and the Professor. Say hello, boys. Heaven is going to be our new countergirl."

Homeys? I struggled to stifle a giggle. This Farnsworth guy was definitely going to be entertaining. Rom and Shigeto – two of the sleek-looking, DJ-spinning kind of kids – rolled their eyes a little, but Rom gave me a little nod and Shigeto smiled and winked at me. Shigeto was the guy who had been speaking Japanese earlier. For a second I panicked – had he recognised me? But in the time it took me to get all worked up about it, he had already turned back to his computer game and resumed blasting away at something. I guessed I was safe. The Professor seemed to be cut from the same cloth as Farnsworth. He was a big-headphoned, dumpy guy with a big smile. He looked as harmless as a puppy.

"What kind of professor are you?" I asked him.

"A professor of the Internet," he said, grinning and offering his hand. *Give me a break.*

"The Professor is our best customer," Farnsworth said proudly. "He's here all the time." I groaned inwardly. Both the Professor and Farnsworth were staring at me with love-struck eyes. Why couldn't Hiro look at me like that?

Farnsworth and I spoke for a little while longer, arranging that my first shift would be tomorrow at one. He gave me a spare set of keys in case I ever had to open up the store in the morning. And he kept thanking me over and over. I left, giving everyone a little wave, and finally found my way out the door.

Standing outside in the brisk air, I looked back into Life Bytes and saw Farnsworth gathered around his homeys, giving everyone a high five. I caught only snippets of what he was saying, but a word that stuck out very clearly was the word *babelicious*. I hadn't heard anyone use that word since . . . ever.

What had I got myself into? I took a deep breath and tried to think calm thoughts. Even though Life Bytes seemed kind of strange, I couldn't help but feel a little proud of myself. I had done something. I had made a change for myself. I had marched in there and negotiated a higher salary – even if only by accident! Way to go, me! If only Hiro could see me now. If only Ohiko could see me now. For once, thinking of Ohiko didn't make me burst into tears. Instead, I felt that he was watching over me – guiding me, even. Ohiko would have got a real kick out of Farnsworth, that was for sure. I walked quickly. Now I was a girl with a purpose. A job. I smiled and felt strong.

This is probably more amazing than the time they came out with the Magic Onslaught cards. Professor and I happened to get to the store before anyone else, and we were able to buy the whole set without wandering around to any other stores or searching on the Internet or anything. I mean, it's probably not the most *wonderful thing – there was that time we were able to sneak into the* Star Wars *triple feature at the Torrence theatre, or there was that time when I went to that garage sale and found vintage X-wing fighters still in the box, so I'm probably overreacting. But still, you should have seen the troglodytes that came in here before this girl did . . . They were beyond Cro-Magnon, mere amoebas, just slug bodies and potato noggins for heads, kind of like pod people. And then this girl – she's gorgeous, this perfect specimen – she comes walking in and she actually wants the job and every-thing actually goes right for once, which never seems to hap-pen with me and my romantic forays. She's like those wild girls in Shonen Knife – she just needs tall kneesocks and a crazy ponytail – but she's more beautiful than them, actually. The Internet dating was a complete bust: I signed on to match.com and even included that picture of myself in a cowboy hat (aren't cowboy hats in style? Bentley had insisted they were, so we set up the Net cam and did the shot and I thought it looked pretty goofy, but Bentley insisted it would be an instant babe magnet) but no one answered. I'm beginning to think there are no girls in this city, or at least no smart girls, and maybe this girl is a smart girl. I wonder if she's into Dungeons and Dragons, or is that too old of a game . . . She seemed to have a little bit of an accent. I wonder how new she is to the country, but she's got her English down pretty well. I could be her Belldandy and she could be the lovely Keiichi (or maybe it's the other way around, I can't remember), and I wanted to get out my X-Ray Specs and get a better view of her insides, although I don't know if they really work or not – I've been too shy to try them on anyone. I could protect her from all the rough characters who come blowing through this neighbourhood – they've left us alone so far, I think because of some of the guys Scott knows – but wouldn't I be the hero if I saved heavenly Heaven from some big burly dude who came sweeping into here acting all tough? But if there's a big bad wolf staking out the old Life Bytes fortress of solitude, I'd better stick around while celestial Heaven is manning the counter. I wouldn't want her alone in here if something ever happened – I see her as the delicate type, a hothouse flower perhaps, completely in need of a rescuer in times of peril. Meaning, yep, you guessed it, old Farnsworth, stud extraordinaire, will have to just nobly put in some extra hours to play bodyguard to my precious orchid. Not such a bad deal all round, I'd say. As Mr Burns from* The Simpsons *says, "Exxxxxcellent, Smithers." Excellent, indeed.*

Farnsworth

5

I walked around aimlessly for a while, just soaking in the sun, feeling like quite the little go-getter. I wished I could call someone, but there was no one to call. Hiro was teaching classes right now. I didn't feel like relaying the news to Karen. If only I knew Katie's phone number in Las Vegas. I'd tried to look it up once before, but there was no listing. But I was pretty sure that was where she lived.

I looked around. Finding a job had gone so swimmingly, I wondered if I should try to make some headway towards finding an apartment. If my apartment search went like my job search, maybe I could find a huge penthouse loft in Beverly Hills with no background check for two hundred dollars a month. Or maybe that was pushing it. But to get out of Karen's house, I would settle for much, *much* less. Karen had said there were apartment listings in the papers. Maybe I could find a place to buy a paper. I started walking.

I walked up Wilshire, checking out the storefronts. I think I was in Echo Park. All kinds of people were coming and going – guys with multicoloured mohawks, people gabbing away on cell phones, women and baby carriages, perfectly toned women carrying yoga mats. Suddenly I noticed the name of a small street jutting out across the avenue. Dawson Street, it said. Why was that name familiar? I felt like I'd seen it before. Had I just walked by it earlier today, or . . .

Duh! This is where Cheryl lives! I looked around with a big smile. Right after my wedding, when I'd been wandering around all bloody and lost, I'd sort of accidentally crashed this party in Hollywood. The party was given by this cool girl named Cheryl, who ended up loaning me some clothes and helping me figure out where Hiro lived. About a week ago, I'd gone to Cheryl's place to return her clothes and wound up on this crazy shop-ping/drinking/dancing trip where I'd ended up kicking the butts of these two jerky guys. It had been an awesome night.

I looked up and down Dawson Street and immediately spotted Cheryl's house. It was a ramshackle yellow number with a big front yard that held a couple of shaggy, undertended palm trees. You could tell young people lived there. An old beat-up car was parked crookedly in the driveway. I took a deep breath and went up to ring the bell.

It took a few minutes for someone to come to the door, and I was beginning to think nobody was home. But just as I was about to leave, the door swung open to reveal Cheryl, her dyed-blonde hair sticking up in a million different directions, wearing an old sweatshirt and little shorts and talking on a cordless phone. She took one look at me and broke into a huge grin. "I'll call you back," she said to whoever she was talking to. She clicked off the phone and let out a whoop. "Oh my God!" she said. "Heaven, my ass-kicking sister! It's so good to see you! Where've you been? We *have* to go out again!"

"Definitely," I said, laughing. "I was just in the neighbourhood. And see? I'm wearing my new clothes!" Cheryl laughed, too. Actually, I was wearing a pair of the tight pants Cheryl had helped me pick out, with a simple hoodie that I'd picked up at the Gap. Most of the stuff I'd bought with Cheryl was a little too party girl to wear out during the day. "Actually," I said, "I was wondering if you wanted to get a cup of coffee or lunch or something."

Cheryl grinned. "Awww, you're too nice. I'd love to. But why don't you come in instead? I was just making tea. Have some with me. We can catch up."

I shrugged. Why not? I smiled and followed Cheryl inside. I thought that some of the stuff I'd seen last time was decoration for the Halloween party, but either Cheryl had been too lazy to take down some of the cobwebs and tribal masks, or they were permanent additions.

We sat down at her kitchen table and Cheryl chattered away about whatever came into her head. Although I was brimming over with my need to tell someone my news about the job, listening to Cheryl was strangely soothing. I guess after being around serious Hiro and cool Karen – and even awkward Farnsworth, for those few minutes – I was a little on edge. Cheryl was upbeat and crazy and supercreative. She seriously lit up the room.

Once we were nearly done with our tea, she looked at me. "So what's happening with your situation?" she asked.

Well, there are people trying to kill me and I'm in love with my trainer, who's dating my temporary roommate, and I seem to be working in a nerd factory for fifteen dollars an hour . . . "A lot," I admitted. "You remember that friend of mine I was staying with?"

"The friend on Lily Place?"

"Yeah, him. Well . . ." I sighed. I needed yet another excuse for moving out of Hiro's house besides *There are some crazy people trying to kill me and I don't want them killing Hiro.* "There's not enough space there," I said finally, "and he's just starting to date this girl, so he needs his privacy. So I've been looking around for another place to live."

Cheryl smiled. "Thinking of hanging around in L.A., then?"

I shrugged. "I guess. I just got a job today that pays fifteen dollars an hour." I smiled shyly.

Cheryl raised her eyebrows and whistled. "Awesome!" she said. "What a score!"

"I think it will be pretty easy work. So yeah, I guess I'll stay."

Cheryl pounded her fist on the table exuberantly, making the teacups shake. "You might be in luck, Heaven. I know someone who's looking for a roommate."

"Really?" I said.

Cheryl nodded. "Can you tolerate noise?" I shrugged. I was a deep sleeper, especially since I'd started training with Hiro. Practise wiped me out. "Are you fairly clean? Apparently this person's last roommate was an absolute slug when it came to pitching in." I nodded. I might not be as neat as Karen, but Hiro had definitely taught me that I was responsible for my own mess. Cheryl wrapped her hands behind her head, satisfied. "Okay, so listen, Heaven. The person looking for a roommate? It's actually me. And I'm kind of freaking out about it, if you want the truth."

"You?"

"Yeah. Me. My roommate, Otto? You might have seen a glimpse of his head last time you were here? He moved out last weekend and announced that he was going to spend a couple of years in Europe. The jerk. It was completely out of the blue! I have no idea how he'll find the money to do it, but whatever. I mean, in a way, I'm glad to be rid of him. The guy was a complete bore and was good for nothing. He didn't even have a job. But I am *strapped* for cash. Seriously. If I don't come up with this month's rent soon, I'm going to have to live in my car or something. And look at this place!" She swooped her arms around, gesturing to the multicoloured wall murals and the crazy mobiles hanging from the ceiling and the eccentric assortment of furniture. "I've spent a while decorating! What would I do with all these chairs? I don't want to go home to live with my mum, Heaven. I would rather *die*, actually. Do you see my dilemma?"

I nodded.

"I *was* going to put an ad in the paper today, but if you want to stay here, that would help me out so much. Plus I know you. You're a kick-ass chick."

Okay, so I was officially proclaiming this day the Best Day

of My Life. All right, all right, maybe that wasn't totally accurate – there wouldn't be people trying to kill me on the Best Day of My Life. So maybe it was only a Pretty Damn Good Day. I couldn't believe my good luck. I'd love to live with Cheryl. I felt comfortable with her. It seemed much safer than moving in with a stranger. Cheryl was completely unconnected with my world. She already thought the Whisper of Death, my family katana, or sword, was a stage prop from a costume, and hadn't batted an eye at the blood-spattered "costume" I'd stumbled through her door in on my wedding night, which happened to be Halloween. I knew I could trust her not to be nosy.

"You're serious?" I asked.

"Yep," Cheryl said. "Rent's five hundred dollars a month."

I did some quick calculations in my head. "Sounds perfect."

We walked into what would be my room – Otto's old room. I remembered it from before: We'd looked up Hiro's address in here. A strange pang hit me; that seemed like so long ago. I hadn't even met Hiro yet. How things had changed! The room was sunny and spare, and Otto had left his bed and dresser. "You can even have your own phone line in here, no big deal," Cheryl said.

I smiled, quite proud of myself. "I'll take it," I said. "In fact, can I move in today?"

"Definitely," Cheryl said. "And let's go out tonight to celebrate!"

When I woke up the next morning after a night of partying with Cheryl, the first thing I noticed was that I was in a real bed. The window next to me held a sweeping view of downtown L.A. I shot up. Where was I? Then I remembered. Cheryl's place. *My* place. Moving around so many times in a couple of days was pretty dizzying.

Cheryl was knocking on my door. "Heaven? Phone call." Then she whispered, "I think it's *Hiro*."

I smiled. Over dinner I'd confessed to her that I had a crush on Hiro and that he'd started to see this other girl. Who I was insanely jealous of. It had been so long since I'd had a girl-friend I felt I could really trust, and Cheryl was a good listener. We even started laughing about it after a while.

My stomach did a little flip when she said Hiro's name. But when I picked up the phone, he sounded angry.

"You scared the hell out of Karen," he said, reverting back to Japanese. I wondered if the Japanese meant that Karen was still there. She was of Japanese descent but had been raised in the United States and didn't speak the language. "She said that you weren't home when she got back. That you left some kind of cryptic note and all your stuff was gone."

"It wasn't a cryptic note," I argued, feeling a flush of guilt. I hadn't meant for it to be cryptic, anyway. "I told her that I'd found a place to live and I'd found a job. That's all. How is that cryptic?" As I said this, I knew I should have waited for Karen to come home to explain it to her myself. But when I'd gone back to Karen's place to gather up my stuff and found that Karen wasn't home, I'd just grabbed my stuff and split. Where was Karen if she wasn't home? A late-night dojo class? Grocery shopping? Not likely. She had to be with Hiro, probably having a crazy make-out date *right then* as I stood there in her living room. I'd felt jealous. Childish, I know. But I didn't want to be in the way, and I certainly didn't want to see her when she got home from the date *I* wanted to be on, starry-eyed and oblivious. So I had quickly grabbed a sheet of paper from Karen's desk and written her a note:

> Karen –
>
> I had good luck today! I found both a job and an apartment. I'm living with someone who's helped me out before, Cheryl. Her phone number is 555-6790. She lives over on Dawson Street. Please tell Hiro that I am fine. I'll tell you everything when I see you next. I've taken my stuff with me. Thanks for a great day yesterday.
>
> – Heaven

If Karen was so worried, why hadn't she called last night? Or had she even come home last night?

Ugh. I *really* wished I hadn't thought of that.

"Why didn't you call me about any of this?" Hiro said.

"It didn't occur to me," I admitted. I knew that sounded inconsiderate. The truth was, I hadn't called him because I'd thought maybe Karen was at his house. And I guess I'd just wanted to avoid the whole thing. It was obvious that I needed to separate myself. I needed to be my own person.

Hiro said, "Well, who is this person you're staying with? I mean, is it someone you just met off the street? Is that *safe*? Why didn't you wait for me to find you someone? I told you I'd take care of it."

"It *is* safe," I interrupted. "I mean, as safe as anyplace is going to be for me. I met Cheryl when I was running from everything happening at my wedding. She's the one who gave me the change of clothes, the one I went out with that night that you . . . got mad at me for. She's the one who led me to you!"

Hiro sighed. "If you're sure you can trust her, fine. Did you have any luck finding a job?"

"As a matter of fact, I did," I said. "It's at a cybercafé, part-time, and it pays fifteen dollars an hour."

Hiro whistled. "I'm impressed," he said. "It's hard to find a job in this city. How did you do all of this stuff in one day?"

"I can take care of myself," I said smugly. Talking to Hiro made me even more proud of myself. It was next to impossible to find a job and an apartment in my situation, but I was just the woman to pull it off.

"I guess you can," he replied. "Good. I want to remind you that our training starts up today. But like I said, we should start meeting in different areas, not just the dojo. How about your house? Does it have room for training?"

I thought about it. Cheryl would be leaving in a couple of minutes for her job at some record store; we'd have some privacy. "I guess," I said, and gave him the address.

"Good," Hiro answered. "I'll be over soon."

Hiro showed up in record time and we got started on our morning aikido. I was feeling a little stiff from being out late last night. Also, I realised, this was the first time that I'd been alone with Hiro since right after the attacks. But quickly after I'd awakened from that strange dream with the kiss and Ohiko and my dead father, he'd rushed me off to Karen's house. It certainly was the first time I had been around him since I found out about Karen. Would he tell me about it? Did I really feel like discussing it? I decided not to bring it up. I didn't feel like talking about any of it.

Apparently he didn't either. We went through our warm-up aiki-taiso movements and then did a few exercises that would prepare us for another attack. We went through some basic Japanese karate moves. First the age zuki, or rising punch, which at first looks like a straight punch, but during execution, the fist arcs upward so that the knuckles are the striking surface. And then the hiza geri, or knee hammer – a quick blow of the knee that can be aimed at the head or the groin. When Hiro announced that I had to attack his groin, I didn't know whether I should laugh or cry. The last thing I wanted to do was kick Hiro in the crotch. Or was it? I didn't want to touch him, actually. This was too hard. Finally he noticed what was probably a strange expression and threw up his hands. "You're not actually going to *do* it, Heaven," he said. "You're just going to go through the motions."

"Right," I said. "I *know*." *Idiot*.

We practised attacks against high kicks, arching kicks, hooking kicks, arm locks. I began to feel dizzy. Only a few days out of practise and I was a complete weakling.

"Okay, let's stop for now," Hiro said. Of course he was barely sweating. Robot. "Let's sit down, Heaven. There's something I want to talk to you about."

What could he want to talk about? My mind started racing.

It must be serious. Did Hiro love me and not Karen? Were he and Karen getting married? Had Karen spilled the beans about my "crush" from Japan? Did Hiro really know I was in love with him? If he confronted me, should I deny everything?

Hiro went on. "I know we just dove right back into practise, but I think it's time to talk about your second mission."

My heart sank. Oh. My second *mission*. Fun.

"I want to give you a little background first," Hiro said. "You know, first off, that the samurai culture grew out of the aristocracy. But there were other types of warriors roving Japan at this time as well. There were the lawless samurai, the ronin, and there were also the ninja. The ninja were an interesting group of people because they tended to be of lower-class descent and adopted the ninja way as a defense against the constant samurai raids of their territory. They tried every trick in the book, including what some surmised to be 'black magic,' basically because the samurai outnumbered them, and they had to survive in any way possible."

Talking about ninjas made me shiver. I thought about the cloaked man at the wedding. I thought about the vaporous figure who had brought down my father.

Hiro continued. "The ninjutsu way is portrayed through plenty of movies as being this renegade, evil power, but we have to understand that they were just trying to defend themselves in any way possible. There are very important things we can learn from the medieval ninja. One, that superior numbers don't necessarily ensure victory. The second thing that we can learn from them is the art of stealth," Hiro said. "Ninjas thrive on the shadows. They're able to use concentration, mind power, and a few simple movements to make themselves completely invisible – or so you think. Really, they've just tricked you into not seeing them. They've developed a heightened sense of haragei, awareness, and have created a sound, unshakable sense of concentration so that they have the utmost dedication to their surroundings and enemies.

"But being invisible isn't the crazy stuff you've seen in *Crouching Tiger, Hidden Dragon* or those Bruce Lee movies," Hiro said, smiling. Of course, that was what I'd been thinking. "That's an exaggeration. It's much more subtle than that. But it's a priceless resource if you can master it. There is a very real philosophy, called the shinobi-iri method, which, if practised, can make you invisible when walking down a crowded street. It can make you invisible when fighting your enemy. It can come to your advantage if you think your enemy is more skilled at combat or stronger than you are. And if there is more than one foe you're up against, it can help you bring them all down."

Great, I thought. Because I was so looking forward to being up against more than one foe.

I led Hiro back into my almost empty bedroom. We went through some of the simple invisibility moves. First was the stealth walk, which was basically a way of walking soundlessly. There was also a camouflage method of holding weapons. "Always hold them close to the body," Hiro explained. "Otherwise your silhouette will give you away."

It sounded too easy. We went over the simple roll as well,

which enabled a person to get across a room faster and much lower to the ground – and thus be less easily detected. We spent about a half hour rolling back and forth across the room. I couldn't help but giggle. I felt like Pikachu, the little yellow Pokémon character.

"This is serious!" Hiro said. His seriousness made me laugh even harder. I almost wanted to make him angry.

We went over what Hiro called the "most important" part of the process: the meditation and mind-control segments. Hiro had us sit down and breathe very evenly for about fifteen minutes. "Tension means weakness," he whispered. "If all five senses are working together and relaxed, you can do anything."

After we finished, Hiro paused and looked at me. "Are you okay, after what happened the other day?"

I almost thought he meant after finding out what I had from Karen, but then I realised he meant after the attack. "Yeah, I think so," I said, trying to sound strong. But inside, just thinking about those thugs made my heart race. I guess it was stupid of me to hope that they were really after my father and that after he returned to Japan, the attacks would stop. They wanted me. What if they traced me to this address? I gritted my teeth. I had to learn more about who was after me.

"Hiro, I—" Before I could finish, his cell phone rang.

Hiro answered it after looking at his caller ID. "Hi, Karen," he said. *Crap.* I stayed very still. Hiro spoke to her for a couple of minutes, not saying much more than "Yeah" and "Okay." (I noticed his voice didn't go all soft the way hers did when talking to him and felt kind of happy about that. But maybe it just wasn't his style.) Finally he said, "Will you lock my apartment when you leave? Okay. Thanks. See you later."

Lock my apartment when you leave? I felt like somebody had punched me in the stomach. *Lock my apartment when you leave?* Karen had spent the night there. That could mean only one thing.

Karen and Hiro were sleeping together.

I thought of how good kissing Hiro had felt in my dream. How warm his skin had felt. How I couldn't get close enough to him.

Apparently Karen felt the same way.

As I was having my internal conniption, Hiro hung up and looked at me. I felt like I was blushing so hard, my face must be purple. Did he know I knew? His face betrayed nothing.

"Karen said that my bike messenger service just called my house and needs me to work a few hours this afternoon. How about this is it for today?"

"Sure," I managed to choke out. "I have to go to work, anyway."

Hiro smiled and gathered up his stuff as I tried to regulate my breathing. *Lock my apartment when you leave?* Thank God I hadn't spent the night at Karen's the night before. It would have killed me to know for sure that she wasn't coming home . . . and why.

"Great work today, Heaven," Hiro said, putting his hand on my arm. "I'll see you tomorrow. I'll call you and let you know where we'll be practising. And remember, start going through those stealth exercises."

"Uh-huh," I muttered. *Right. Stealth.* "See you." He shut

the door and walked down the slope to where he'd parked his bike.

As he left, I turned back to my empty bedroom and tried to calm the frantic feeling in my stomach. *Distance,* I thought. *Distance yourself, Heaven.* But still, I felt like someone had stuck an ice pick in my heart.

How ironic, I thought, *that my new mission is to become invisible.* Just when I wanted Hiro to really *see* me.

Another hour of meditation is the only answer. I have much to think about. I sit on my mat and breathe in and out. I try to release the negative ki within me. I release one by one my five weaknesses. First anger, dosha. I let it flutter out of me. Next fear, kyosha. I feel a buildup of strength within my body. I fear nothing. Next lust, kisha.

Lust is harder. I know the bushi way is to keep lust under control. Lust means weak-willedness. It means you are unbalanced.

Karen is so composed and patient. She is a lotus flower. I try to keep my emotions in control around her, but sometimes it is difficult. Sometimes I can't believe my good fortune.

It has been a strain, however, because I haven't told Heaven about it. There were times this week when I wanted to, when I tried, but somehow I couldn't get the words out. There would be times when our eyes would meet, and the scenes from Heaven's life would flash through my head – how we had to abandon her father when he was knocked unconscious. Her story of the tragic wedding. The death of her brother. I am filled with grief for the so many terrible things that have happened to her in the last months.

But it's more than that. There's something else, something that I can't quite put my finger on. We agreed that it would be best if she moved out, but the house is so empty without her. So . . . different. Well timed, of course, because of Karen. But different.

Karen told me she'd said something about us to Heaven. I asked, without trying to sound too eager, "How did she take it?" Karen shrugged and said, "Good, I guess. She has her own things to think about."

I think of Heaven sitting on the couch, in the face of adversity, making me laugh over a silly joke. I'm nervous about her moving away. What if something happens to her?

In, out. In, out. I do a few easy stretches and try to clear my mind. But I can't. There are these two women, one the black of the yang, the other the white of the yin. If I lose one, will I lose my balance?

Hiro

6

"Good morning!" Farnsworth said, beaming, as I walked into Life Bytes later that day. I wondered if he was just happy that I'd shown up. It wasn't like he had any contact info on me, so he was really taking a leap of faith in assuming I'd be there that morning.

The atmosphere of the place was identical to the day before, except there were different guys at the computer terminals, and a slightly different acid house song was on the stereo. But the Professor was still in the corner with his big headphones on. He perked up when he saw me. "Hello, milady!" he said, and then blushed. The other customers glanced up, then quickly back to their screens.

"Um, what should I do?" I asked Farnsworth.

"Just go behind the counter and I'll show you," he said. He crashed into the counter; I could tell he was nervous. "This is the counter," he said. "You'll be manning this . . . or, um, *womanning* this, whenever there's a customer."

Womanning. Right. He walked over to the two huge coffee tureens. "Decaf and caf coffee," he explained. "This one's name is Xena" – he pointed to the one with the black top – "and this one's name is Gabrielle."

I almost burst out laughing. Katie had been weirdly fascinated with the Xena show and brought over videos for us to watch. She'd tried to get me into it, but I'd found it totally goofy. Not my kind of show. But I could see he was dead serious.

Farnsworth showed me some other items on the counter. I was relieved to see that it was kept fairly clean. Actually, the coffee mugs were kind of cool – almost futuristic looking. The guys at the computers tapped away at a million miles a minute. After a few more directions, Farnsworth left me on my own at the counter and headed into the back room to finish some paperwork.

I stood behind the counter and looked blankly out the window. In the time Farnsworth had shown me around, no one had come in.

A young Asian kid in a bright yellow Adidas track jacket approached the counter. "Hey," he said. "You remember me? Shigeto?" He smiled. I remembered that he'd freaked me out by speaking Japanese the day before, but now he looked pretty harmless. He had a nice, open face – he seemed like a happy guy.

"Sure," I said with a smile. "And I'm Heaven. What can I get for you?"

"Another coffee?" Shigeto thrust his mug out at me. I dutifully grabbed Xena and filled up his cup. This job was *way* too easy.

"Thanks," Shigeto said, taking his mug back. "So, are you here every day now?"

"Only four days a week to start."

"Cool." Shigeto sipped his coffee and grimaced. "*Damn!* Maybe you can convince Farnsworth back there to invest in some better coffee. This stuff tastes like mud."

I shrugged. "I can try, I guess. Maybe he'll upgrade to Starbucks or something."

Shigeto nodded. "Now you're talking."

I rested my elbows on the counter and laughed. Actually, Shigeto was kind of cute. I tried to think of something else to say, but my mouth felt all awkward, like I'd never spoken before or something. Then I looked up at his face. He had this easy, mild smile, like he was just the friendliest guy in the world. Suddenly I didn't feel so awkward. "So, you're one of Farnsworth's homeys?"

To Shigeto's credit, he didn't even look embarrassed. He gave a little chuckle and nodded. "That's right. I've known Farnsworth for years. We went to school together at UCLA." Shigeto sipped his coffee and made another face. "He's a great guy, really. Got a heart of gold."

Suddenly the Professor called from the other side of the room. "Shigeto, you better come over here," he said. "I've got the download of the one of the new Xbox fighting games!"

"Awesome," Shigeto said. "You're kidding."

"I hacked into the system," the Professor explained.

Shigeto turned to me and grinned. "Well, duty calls," he

said airily. "I'm glad you're going to be working here. You'll definitely class up this joint."

I leaned back and smiled. "Thanks!" Shigeto headed back to the computer terminals. *Now, there's a nice guy,* I thought as I put Xena back on her warmer and grabbed a rag to wipe off the counter. *Why can't Hiro be more like that? Cheery. Easy to talk to. Easy to understand.* My mind wandered back to his phone call with Karen that morning . . . how she'd stayed at his place. I realised that the night before was only the second night I'd been out of Hiro's house and the first night Karen had stayed there. Suddenly a horrible feeling washed over me. Had he just been waiting for me to leave so he could move in on Karen? My stomach lurched. I remembered that moment making dinner a few days ago, the moment I'd been so sure he was going to say he had feelings for me. Maybe what he'd wanted to say was more like, "Hey, would you mind getting lost for a night?" I felt nauseous. It sounds stupid, but I'd kind of believed Hiro was better than that. Not that he didn't have desires, like everyone. But he'd seemed so noble, like he could hold all of his desires in check . . . until the right moment. The right, fabulous, fabulous moment.

Stop it, Heaven, I thought, reining my imagination back in. *I should forget about him. At least in* that *way.*

Shigeto and some other kids gathered around the computer terminal. I noticed some other guy was watching a movie download – it looked like *Gladiator* – on the Internet. It had been a long time since I'd used the Internet myself. Hiro didn't have it at his house; the last time I'd used it had been to find

Hiro's address at Cheryl's. I wasn't supposed to use it in Japan. My father had been too strict. Katie had a laptop, and we snuck on sometimes and watched world premieres of videos and surfed into stupid chat rooms, and I even had an e-mail pen pal from Australia for about a week. But then Konishi had found out because Mieko had "accidentally" let it slip. Of course my Internet use had ended right then and there. I wondered if Cheryl had an Internet connection at home now that her roommate was gone; probably not. I kind of remembered that it was his computer we were using.

I thought a little more about this. I wondered if the Internet could give me any clues about who was after me. Where could I start? It wasn't like someone was going to post, *I'm after Heaven Kogo, ha ha!* on a chat room site or something.

But then there was my father. All the secrets he was keeping. The attack at the restaurant that had left him comatose – an attack that might have been aimed at either one of us. Say those thugs *were* after my father all along. Say it was bad business blood; a deal gone wrong and my father was to blame. Frankly, I had no *idea* what my father did for a living. I had some concerns about it – I mean, my father wasn't always a very nice guy, especially in matters concerning his "business" – but no hard facts. Kogo Industries might be a ring of serial killers or a Hello Kitty distributor. All I knew was that every morning, Konishi would disappear into his office on the other side of our compound. Sometimes we wouldn't see him until dinnertime. Sometimes we wouldn't see him for days.

It made sense that I could use the Internet to figure out

74

what kind of business my father did. And depending on what I found out, that information could lead to who was after us.

I went up to Farnsworth, who was working on another computer. "Do you mind if I, um, use the computers when there aren't any customers?"

Farnsworth nodded eagerly. "Of course, that's fine," he said. "Just make sure to get back to the counter when you're needed." It didn't look like that would be very often, but I didn't say anything.

I got straight to work. The Professor floated over and stood over me. "Need any help?" he said. "I do know quite a bit about the Internet." He blushed a little. Weirdly enough, he looked smug and kind of embarrassed at the same time.

I minimised my screen. "Uh, no, I think I can manage," I said. Then I smiled. "I'll let you know if I do, though."

He smiled back and walked away.

I opened up a window with the MTV web site to throw them off and opened a smaller window where I would do my search. I immediately typed in KONISHI KOGO to google.com. Quite a few listings popped up. Links to his business web site, links to major newspaper references, links to interviews. But I wanted the dirt, the gossip. The stuff that wasn't necessarily true and wasn't found in the most reputable of resources but had some street credibility to it. I guess I knew what to look for from all of the crime investigation movies I'd watched. I was looking for the underground viewpoint.

Then an article came up, buried on the eighth page of search results. It was titled "Rumours of Kogo Industry Empire."

I hungrily clicked on it. I skimmed the text, glossing over the background information about my father and his work. And then I came upon a sentence that I hadn't exactly anticipated.

Kogo Industries is rumoured to have very strong yakuza connections.

I felt like my heart literally stopped.

Yakuza.

The Japanese mafia.

I felt like I had to be shaking, even though the customers around me didn't seem to notice anything amiss. I felt my face grow hot. The yakuza were criminals, killers, drug lords. I almost felt ready to throw up. Had my father ever . . . *killed* anyone? Did he only have connections to the yakuza . . . or was he yakuza himself?

I closed the screen and took a few deep breaths.

I did a few other searches on the yakuza in general. The *mafia*. The Chinese *Triads*. Extortions, killings, prostitution, rigging of big industries, illegal gambling, torturing.

This was what my father did for a living. Or if he didn't do it himself, he worked with people who did.

My father. The same man who'd held me on his lap when I was a little girl, reading me stories. The same man whose hugs, when I was little, could always stop my crying. Has those same hands . . . *killed* someone? Was it possible that the father I loved and . . . honestly, feared . . . had been hurting innocent people every *day* of my childhood?

Finally I just couldn't take any more. I closed the window where I was conducting my research and was faced once again with the MTV web site. Completely oblivious to the terrifying information I had just received, Carson Daly grinned up at me vapidly.

I shut his window, too.

Slowly I backed my chair away from the computer and stood. Shigeto turned from the computer where he was playing the Professor's Xbox games and smiled. "Done playing around, huh?" he asked.

"Yeah." I tried to smile, but I don't think I succeeded. I walked stiffly back over to my counter and stared out the window.

I was done playing around. And all of my research had told me only one thing.

I didn't really know my father at all.

7

Time seemed to pass quickly at Life Bytes. Which was strange, because it wasn't like I was *doing* much. But for some reason just hanging out at the counter, playing the occasional game of Minesweeper, and talking to all the regulars felt *right*. It calmed me down, even after the bombshell I had just received. For the time being, at least, I was just a regular person doing her job.

Not some freak mafia daughter who was barely outrunning her killer father.

Late that afternoon, about an hour before my shift ended, someone walked through the front door. Actually, he was the first person to walk through the door all day. This new guy was tall, with spiky black hair and a gold tooth. He looked different from the others in the place – more "street," somehow. More dangerous. He wore a gigantic ring on his thumb. "Coffee, black," he ordered, scanning the room.

I filled his coffee, my hands quivering. Something about

this guy set me on edge, and I couldn't quite put my finger on it.

He stood at the counter and slowly sipped his coffee, looking around at the computers. I stood awkwardly, not sure what to do with my hands. Farnsworth was hovering over some kid's computer in the back, probably still playing a video game. The front doorbells jingled and another guy walked in. I felt myself blushing almost – he was gorgeous. He wore a leather jacket and was tall and lean. He walked up to the guy at the counter and they gave each other a weird handshake. His face was angular and he had these gorgeous cheekbones. I studied him carefully. He looked Japanese.

He saw me behind the counter and broke into a smile. "Hey," he said.

"Hey," I said, and smiled back. "What can I get for you?"

"Hmm." He studied the menu. His friend leaned against the counter, bored, and then wandered off to one of the computers. "A coffee, I guess. Heavy on the milk."

"Right," I said. If Shigeto was cute, this guy was *hot*. I thought briefly of Hiro and then pushed the picture of him out of my mind. *Forget Hiro,* I reminded myself. *You're invisible to him. You can make this guy see you.* He was different from the regulars, too – he had sort of a dangerousness about him. I had a feeling that if Hiro saw me talking to him, he'd get upset – and not because he was jealous. Because this wasn't the kind of person I should associate with. He had a slick suaveness that didn't seem quite real. He seemed like trouble.

But *damn*. It was high time I got to flirt with someone!

"Here you go," I said, handing him his mug. He winked at me, and I smiled. That was when I noticed it.

He was missing a finger.

The colour drained from my face, and I quickly turned around to face the coffee tureens. When a yakuza henchman did something to upset the big boss, the only way to regain his favour was to prove your loyalty by cutting off a finger. It was like a mini act of seppuku, ritual suicide. I shuddered, picturing the tiny stump in my mind. This guy was yakuza.

Then I had a scary thought.

What if he knows my father?

What if he's here because of me?

I turned around. Truth be told, it didn't seem like the guy was paying any attention to me. He had his hands in his pockets and was talking in fast Japanese to the other guy. They were talking about meeting up with some girls later or something – I couldn't quite tell, since they were talking in such low voices. I breathed out.

Maybe I could *make* him pay attention to me. And learn a few things from him. If I played my cards right.

The guy turned back to me and smiled. He'd drained his coffee cup. "You mind if I have a little more?" he asked.

"No problem," I said, trying to smile. He handed his mug back, and I poured him a cup from Xena. I straightened up and handed him the coffee.

"Thanks," he said.

"You're welcome," I said in Japanese. The guy's eyes lit up. He broke into a lazy smile.

"Where are you from?" he asked, also in Japanese.

"Tokyo," I said, running my fingers through my hair and staring right into his eyes. I totally didn't know whether I was doing this right. All of my information on flirting came from soap operas and *90210* reruns.

But the guy seemed to respond, leaning in so that I could smell the leather of his coat. "Yeah?" he said. "Where in Tokyo?"

"Oh, around," I said. If he started asking too many questions, I might inadvertently give something away. "So what's your name?" I looked directly at his missing finger.

He looked down, too. "My name's Yoshitomo," he said softly. He looked up at me. I could see what he was thinking in his eyes. *You know what that means?*

Before I could stop myself, I made myself say, "I'm really attracted to the dangerous type." I couldn't believe these words were coming out of my mouth. I lowered my voice to what I hoped was a breathy, Jessica Rabbit–style pitch.

"My life's pretty dangerous, all right," Yoshitomo said.

"Oh, I bet you're not *always* dangerous," I said, winding a strand of my hair around my finger. "You look like you could be very . . . gentle . . . too." I looked up at him from underneath my eyelashes. It looked like I'd hit a bull's-eye.

"I can definitely be gentle . . . with the right lady," he said with a little gleam in his eye. He moved his hand over the counter and lightly ran a finger down my arm. I tried to keep from flinching. I was turned on and terrified at the same time. A very strange and electrifying combination. "You like dangerous?" he went on, in a low voice like a tiger's purr. "You don't even know what I've had to do, little girl," he said. "You wouldn't want to."

"I have an idea," I said softly, looking into his eyes.

Yoshitomo raised his eyebrows and leaned in, resting his hand on mine. I could feel the scarred skin that covered his missing finger. His eyes seemed darker now. "You do, huh?" he asked, smiling to reveal a set of glaringly white teeth. He looked almost wolfish for a minute. And I felt very Little Red Riding Hood. "How would a pretty thing like you know anything about the world I live in?"

"I . . . my brother," I said, before I could think it through. *Oh, forgive me, Ohiko, I know you would never . . .* But that seemed like the only way I might believably be connected to the yakuza. "He worked for . . . for a very important man."

"He did?" Yoshitomo frowned for a moment, looking serious. He looked me over doubtfully. "What happened to him?" he asked me in a surly whisper.

For the first time since I'd entered Life Bytes, I felt afraid. *Please, please let this work.* "He got messed up in some bad business," I went on in my breathy whisper. Now I was so scared, I didn't have to work very hard to sound breathy. "You know . . ." I looked into his black eyes. ". . . the business with Konishi Kogo."

At the mention of my father's name, Yoshitomo's eyes widened, and all the blood left my face. Everything I'd suspected was confirmed in his expression. "Konishi Kogo?" he whispered. "That's some bad business, all right. Your brother worked for him?"

Worked for him. Worked *for* him. My father was a yakuza boss. All the breath left my body, but I forced myself to stay focused. I was about to say yes, but instead I was hit by a flash of inspiration. "Not for him," I whispered. "For . . . his rival."

Yoshitomo nodded sagely. "The Yukemuras," he whispered.

A chill ran down my spine. *The Yukemuras. Of course. His "business" rivals.* "Yes," I managed to choke out. My whole world was spinning. *Everything I've ever believed about my family was a lie.*

Yoshitomo shook his head sympathetically and placed his stubby hand on mine again, bringing me back to the present. "The Yukemuras . . . they're into some wack stuff. Dangerous," he whispered. "Some of the things they do . . . They are the worst of the worst."

I nodded. "I . . . I know." *The worst of the worst. And I was almost married into them. Why? Why would my father do that to me – especially if they were enemies?*

"Kogo is in a bad way," Yoshitomo went on. "He is in a coma now, and people say it's because of a double cross within his own gumi."

"I heard that," I lied, still trying to be flirty, although now I didn't feel like it at all. *A double cross within his own gumi?* So my father was the "boss," and one of his men had betrayed him? It was too much information to take in all at once. I felt like my heart would explode.

Yoshitomo frowned. "I'm sorry to hear about your brother," he said, pulling his hand away. "This isn't something for a girl as young as you to know."

I tried to smile. "But I'm a different kind of young girl," I said.

"I see that," he said, looking me up and down.

Konishi was the *boss*. Like . . . like Tony Soprano, Vito Corleone? But he wasn't anything like those guys — I couldn't even allow the idea to sink in properly. Everything washed over me as if I were a sheet of ice. Hopefully Yoshitomo didn't see how shocked I was. "Do they know who double-crossed Konishi?" I croaked.

He shook his head. "He had many enemies. But I shouldn't be getting into this," he said. "What's your story?"

"Oh. Uh . . . boring stuff. I'm here to go to school," I lied.

Tony Soprano. My father *was* Tony Soprano, whether he looked like him or not. For a second I had this weird vision of myself as bratty Meadow, Ohiko as sullen A. J., Mieko as disapproving Carmela. I almost laughed, it seemed so ridiculous. Mieko was about as un-Carmela as a person could possibly get. But when I thought about it, I could see the similarities between our family and the Sopranos. Hanging around in our fancy house, wearing our fancy clothes, driving our fancy cars, and the whole time all that money was coming from other people's blood. *I never knew*.

I looked up at the guy, who was still smiling at me, slowly sipping his coffee. "Have you ever . . . killed anybody?" I whispered. The question came out before I could think about it. As soon as the words left my mouth, I wondered if it was the wrong thing to ask.

He flinched and looked sort of uncomfortable, then tried to

pass it off with a smile. "Why?" he said, not answering my question. "Do you need protecting?"

I shook my head. "I can fend for myself," I said. I'd definitely done enough of that in the last few weeks. "And I still think you're a big pussycat."

He shook his head, laughing. "You're a strange girl."

We locked eyes – and then his cell phone rang. He rummaged around his coat pocket to get it. After a brief conversation he motioned for his friend.

He looked back at me. "It was nice meeting you," he said. "What was your name?"

"Karen," I said. It was the only name I could think of.

He gave me a crooked, gorgeous smile and then rushed away.

I put my hands on my temples. My head spun. Konishi Kogo, yakuza boss. Yoji Yukemura, his rival boss. My whole life had been paid for by yakuza blood money. My father was a worse man than I ever could have imagined.

And Ohiko. His banishment from our lives. Suddenly it all made so much sense. Had he refused to join my father's "business"? In my naiveté, I'd thought that Ohiko simply didn't want to work at Kogo Industries. *Baka!* I thought. How stupid could I have been? Of course. Ohiko hadn't wanted to become an initiated member of the yakuza. Of course Ohiko wouldn't stoop to that! He probably refused and was cast out of my family! I remembered the day when Ohiko "disappeared." My father wouldn't speak about it . . . at all. Of course! He didn't want to admit that he was trying to drag Ohiko into the underworld of crime. Ohiko was training to become a samurai as well and had been much further in training than I was now. He was much too noble and pure of mind to ever accept the yakuza way. Certainly no self-respecting samurai would consider yakuza dealings acceptable within the code of bushido.

I realised my hands were clenched into fists. Yoshitomo had said my father had many enemies. I assumed he'd meant enemies in the yakuza world. And my father had said Ohiko had gone to work with an "enemy," which now I interpreted as another yakuza gumi, or family. But would Ohiko do something like that? Why?

I walked back to the computer, opened up the Sanrio Hello Kitty site as a distraction, and typed OHIKO KOGO into the search engine and looked for any yakuza-related chat rooms.

Nothing.

I sat at the computer, dumbstruck. I thought about the parties my father had held at our house. I was never allowed to go to any of them for more than a second. Katie and I would hole up in my bedroom, watching movie after movie, having a grand old time. The thought of what might have been going on downstairs now made me a little sick. But I remembered plenty of politicians and businessmen attending the party as well. Was everyone in Japan connected to yakuza?

I stared blankly at the last web site I had opened up, an informational web site about the yakuza in general. *The yakuza are trying to convince the rest of Japan that they are the world's modern-day samurai, the champions of the poor, loyal to the family code,* I read.

Family code? And what would that be? Prostitution, drug running, killing? If my father had given that line to Ohiko, no doubt he laughed in his face.

I pressed print on some of the pages I'd found. I wanted to hold on to them and study them longer; I'd skimmed many of them quickly because I didn't want anyone at Life Bytes to see what I was doing.

I sighed as the printer whirred into action. What was the "dangerous stuff" the Yukemuras were involved in? Maybe the seedier side of crime? Like drugs? I wondered if my father was involved in drugs. Oh God. *Drugs.* He was so *antidrug* where Ohiko and I were concerned. He got all nervous when we took *aspirin.* I began to get angry. What a hypocrite! What a nasty, disgusting, deceiving hypocrite!

I took a couple of deep breaths. I thought again of the Yukemuras, the family I'd almost joined. My father had always told me that the marriage was a business arrangement. An arrangement to unite the two yakuza families? In some kind of truce? I'd known since I was a little kid that my father and Yoji Yukemura merely "tolerated" each other when doing business. They were more or less enemies. I was never allowed to play with Teddy growing up (not that I'd ever wanted to). But if they hated each other so much, why marry us?

I wondered. What if the Yukemuras, esteemed for their dangerousness, had somehow set up the wedding as a "truce" but then double-crossed my father on my wedding day? What if the Yukemuras had planted the lie in my father's head about Ohiko? What if they were the ones who were after us?

I had to say, it made a lot of sense.

A shiver travelled down my back. My almost-husband's family could be behind this whole thing.

"What are you working on?" a voice came behind me. It was the Professor this time. I minimised my screen and blushed. Now the only screen that was up was the Hello Kitty web site. Cat cartoons waved happily.

"Awww," the Professor said.

But then I wondered. Perhaps these guys could help me. They seemed to know everything about electronics. There were a few things I needed; I wondered if they knew where I could find them.

So I took a deep breath and asked the Professor to sit down. "I'm working on something that's a little weird," I said quietly. "I'm trying to find out the truth about someone I'm associated with. It could get me into some trouble. I don't want him to know that I'm looking up stuff on him. Do you know if there's any way I can do things invisibly, like search the Internet without leaving a trace that I've been to a particular chat room or make phone calls without my name coming up?"

"Sure," he said. "I have a friend who works for a big cell phone company. They're developing something called a dis-posable cell phone. You use it once or twice, you throw it away. It's supposed to be for people on vacation or something, but it's also good for people who don't want to be traced. I'll see if I can get you a couple."

"That would be great," I said.

"And Internet searching . . . well . . . there's a code you type in if you don't want your search path to be tracked." He wrote down the code on a piece of paper and handed it to me. "There's untraceable e-mail, too. Again, it's kinda like the untraceable cell phone. You sign up with a search provider, put in the code that won't track where you're going, and get a new e-mail address. Don't fill in any of your real information. There's enough e-mail providers out there these days that are free and don't care. Use the address once, then get a new one."

"Okay," I said. "Great. Thanks." I had a hunch these guys would know their stuff.

The Professor turned to go back to his computer and then turned around again. "So, who's the guy?" he asked.

"What?" I said.

He smiled. "Well, I'm guessing you want to check up on a boyfriend, right? See if he's messing around? That's why you don't want to be traced, right?"

I nodded shakily. "Uh, yeah. That's why."

But something in my expression must have told him that what I was dealing with was much bigger and much scarier than an unfaithful boyfriend. He backed away, looking concerned, his sly smile gone. "Well, whatever help you need, I'll be here, no questions asked."

By then darkness had fallen and I realised my shift was over. I was definitely ready to go home. My first workday had been every bit the struggle I had been expecting – but for completely unexpected reasons. I said goodbye to Farnsworth and the others, slid my coat and glasses on, and slipped outside.

I felt more lost than ever now. Nothing made sense. I had

to collect myself even to find my way home. But I planned to do more of the same tomorrow. I wanted to find out more of my father's dealings with the Yukemuras. Something about that didn't seem quite right. I wanted to see if there were any chat rooms about the wedding arrangements, why they had been made.

I slammed the door. The house was still dark; I guessed Cheryl was still at her job. I threw my coat on a chair and slumped down on the couch, rubbing my temples. I was planning to do more of the invisibility exercises Hiro had taught me, but I felt way too exhausted. Visions of those web sites swam before my eyes.

Then I remembered. I'd printed them out. I'd never picked them up.

"Ughhh," I moaned. Although the Life Bytes boys seemed harmless, I didn't want them to see what I was working on. I didn't want them to know my background. What if they had already picked them up off the printer? Even though they seemed perfectly oblivious and kind, I couldn't trust anybody. I had to go back and get them. It didn't matter if the place was closed – Farnsworth had given me keys.

At least the walk back there would give me a chance to practise my invisibility again. Visions of the people my father might have killed floated before my eyes. I remembered one guy really clearly. A squat guy named Tomo. He was like a Japanese John Candy – really roly-poly, cracking jokes all the time. He had a big, booming voice and would strut down towards the sound-proof compound with my father, chomping on a cigar. Whenever

I saw him, he would have something for me – candy, a flower, a necklace. My father would shake his head, saying, "Tomo, you don't need to buy gifts for my daughter," but Tomo would crinkle up his eyes and say, "But she's beautiful! Everyone should give her gifts!" This was back when I was about twelve, and I loved the attention. My father never called me beautiful.

But then I began to notice that Tomo hadn't come around for a while. One night at dinner I asked my father, "What happened to Tomo?" Mieko had made a little cough, then hid her expression behind a napkin. My father had continued to eat silently. I couldn't understand why he wouldn't answer. I was still his little princess, and he thought all my questions were adorable. "Did he move away?"

"Tomo is not working for me any longer," my father had said. Then he returned to his meal. He said the words in such a way that they ended the conversation.

Did Konishi kill Tomo?

The thought made my stomach crawl. It just didn't seem right – but then nothing I'd learned that day seemed right. Had my father done the killing, or had he hired men to do it for him? I couldn't believe I was having such thoughts. I supposed that Ohiko, once he'd found out (I was certain he knew way more than me, especially since my father was trying to groom him for the business), must have had similar nightmarish thoughts. If only I could have talked with him about it.

At least sliding in and out of the shadows was fun. I was practising the invisibility and doing a pretty good job at it. No one looked me in the eye the whole way to Life Bytes. But when I rounded the corner, I noticed a dark figure standing right in front of the closed Life Bytes. I stopped short, still reeling from the tension of the day. I was too far away to make him out clearly. *Who the hell is that?*

He was holding on to the bars that covered the windows, peering in and then darting his head back and forth. He didn't look the right body type to be Farnsworth or any of the "regulars" I'd hung with that day. Was I crazy, or was he casing the joint to break in? When he turned, I suddenly realised that he was wearing a ski mask.

In L.A.

He was definitely up to something shady.

I thought about all of Farnsworth's stuff in there. The stereo itself was incredible – it had to be worth thousands of dollars. This guy looked like your typical street thug, the kind I'd seen all too much of lately. I didn't want him messing with the place I'd just got a job at. I didn't want him ripping off all of Farnsworth's stuff. And I could probably take him.

I felt adrenaline surge through my body – partly from the success at my first taste of being on my own, partly from the sense that I needed to get this guy away from the store.

So I rushed him.

With quick reflexes I gave him a chop to his neck and immediately drew myself inward for protection, as Hiro had taught me. The man, obviously hurt, wheeled around in pain. Then, with dread, I saw the silvery glint of a knife in his left hand. I hadn't thought that he would be armed. I should have knocked it out of his hands instead of going for his throat. It was a deadly mistake.

Although pained, the man found me and grabbed me by the throat. I tried to get out of the hold, but I couldn't. I'd been taken off guard. I was mesmerised by the knife. He held it to my throat; the metal dug deeper and deeper into my skin.

I was going to be killed by a random street thug for one stupid mistake. I'd never find out the truth about what had happened to Ohiko and wouldn't be there when and if my father recovered from his coma. I'd never find out who was after me. I couldn't even scream.

But then, out of nowhere, the hold on my neck slackened. The knife fell to the man's side. He took me by the shoulder and spun me around. "Heaven? Heaven Kogo?" he asked in an amazed voice.

He lifted up his ski mask, and a chill ran down my back. Nausea gripped my stomach.

I was looking at the face of Teddy Yukemura.

8

Seeing Teddy was like seeing a ghost. He stood nearly a foot taller than me and looked like he'd put on some weight. In other words, he looked like he could beat me to a bloody pulp. His already slimy hair was slicked back and he wore a grubby black hooded sweatshirt. I could see what looked like the inkings of a tattoo poking out from under his sleeve, snaking up his arm. Out of self-defense and fear, I reached up my hand and tried to punch him in the face.

"Hey!" Teddy said, catching my arm and holding it there. I wrenched my arm out from his grip. He stood back and looked at me with this stupid grin. "Wow, check you out! You look fly, girl! What've you been doing with yourself up in this place?"

"Why were you waiting here? Were you waiting to kill me?" I demanded, my eyes flashing. Although my voice rang out steady and certain, inside I was shaking.

"Of course not!" Teddy said. "I was waiting here to talk to you!" He seemed to be studying me intensely, searching every little crevice of my body. It actually felt a little slimy. *Oh my God,* I thought. *Is Teddy checking me out?*

I narrowed my eyes. "Were you going to wait all night? It's *dark* in there. How did you know where to find me?"

Teddy shrugged. "An acquaintance of mine told me that you were here. Said you were acting strange, kind of suspicious. He looked up your picture after he left and realised it was definitely you. So he called me about it."

God, I was such an *idiot!* "Yoshitomo," I breathed, feeling utterly stupid. So much for my subtle sex kitten act. What the hell was wrong with me? I obviously had a lot to learn.

"Who's Yoshitomo?" Teddy asked, frowning.

"Your associate, right?" I demanded. "The guy who called to tell you about me? He came into the café this afternoon."

Teddy shook his head. "I don't know any Yoshitomo," he said. "The guy who called me is in there a lot. Name's Shigeto. He said you were looking up some weird stuff on the Internet."

My stomach dropped into my shoes. Sweet, open Shigeto. God. I couldn't trust anyone, ever.

Teddy gripped me by the shoulders. "Heaven, what are you doing? Why are you hanging out here? Why are you looking up your father on the *Internet*?" Teddy looked up at Life Bytes's rickety sign and the sad, small lights of Chinatown blinking in the distance. Life Bytes was about as far as you could get from the lush surroundings we'd both grown up in.

"None of your damn business! Now leave me alone before I scream!" I said, wondering who would hear me if I did. The street was deserted. I hadn't even seen a car go by once. I lunged for Teddy again, burying a blow into his side. He jumped back and then held my shoulders. He towered over me and anger flashed in his eyes. I don't know why, but I stopped. My whole body shook – it was then I realised how terrified I was. I equated Teddy with death. I was *on the run from him*. It could be Teddy behind all these mysterious thugs attacking Hiro and me. And here he was, right in front of me, tall and horrible and carrying a knife. *The Yukemuras are the worst of the worst.* I shuddered. My breathing was short and nervous. I glared at him and tried to wrench myself from his grip.

"Heaven, control yourself!" Teddy said in a large, some-what terrifying voice. His hands on my shoulders dug deep. I wriggled around, but that made him even angrier. "Listen to me!" he said. "I just want to talk to you! I've just been trying to find you because I think you've misunderstood my role in all of this . . . mess." He took my hands in his. I made a face and wrenched them free.

"Did you send some big guys out to find me a couple of days ago?" I demanded. "Guys who practically gave me brain damage?" *Teddy's in the yakuza,* I thought. *Teddy could kill you. He's probably killed tons of people.*

Teddy shook his head. "Of course not! But that's why we should stick together. You're in a lot of danger being alone, Heaven. I'm your friend. I don't know what's going on, but

96

together we could try to find some of it out. I had nothing to do with what happened on our wedding day. Honest."

"Ha!" I said. "Why should I believe you?"

"You just should," he said, staring at me, practically shaking me. "I can get us both protection. You can trust me, Heaven, I swear. I want to help you."

I averted my eyes and stared off down the empty street. "No, thanks," I said. "I can get by on my own."

"Where are you staying? Can I call you?"

"I'm not telling you that, baka, you idiot," I said. "How stupid do you think I am?"

"Heaven, come on. I'm not your enemy. You've got to believe me. I want to help you. You could be in great danger, but I can get us both protection."

"You already said that," I said.

He pulled out a little scribbled-on piece of paper. "This is where I'm staying," he said. "It has my phone number and address. I can help you, Heaven. At least take my information." He wrenched open my palm and thrust the piece of paper into it. I stared at my hand, as if it had just been overtaken by aliens. I noticed that my hand was shaking.

"Why don't you come with me right now?" Teddy asked. "How safe do you think you'll be even going back to where you're staying? How safe will you be tomorrow?"

"Is that a threat?" I said fiercely. I shoved his phone number and address into my pocket. My hands curled into fists.

"No," Teddy said. "I just want you to be safe." He took my arm and tried to pull me in the direction of the street.

97

"Get away from me!" I said, feeling Teddy's pull. This had to be a setup. Suddenly I remembered a flipping move Hiro had taught me a couple of weeks ago. I stepped back, planted my legs, straightened my arms, and lifted Teddy up. He weighed a ton, and I only half believed it when I felt his body rise into the air and flop over onto the street. I'd actually flipped him.

On his back he wheezed, unable to breathe. "Stay away from me," I said, and slipped into a shadow and started to run.

I ran faster than I ever had before. The trees and the streets were blurs. The few cars on the road were moving slower than my running pace. Once I ran up the driveway of Cheryl's house, I quickly opened the door and closed it behind me, breathing hard.

And then I lost it.

"Oh my God," I sobbed to myself, dissolving into a mess of tears. *So much for strong Heaven.* My whole body shook. I worried that I was going through shock, so I sat down and put my head between my legs. "Oh my God," I said again. Teddy had found me. What if it were his family who were behind all these attacks, all these horrible things that had happened? Had I just narrowly escaped from my murderer? "Oh my God," I whispered again.

The house was still quiet. I didn't know what to do. I tried to watch TV, but all I could think about was Teddy's huge, dirty, snarling face. I crawled into bed but kept one eye open all night, frozen with fear that someone was going to break through my window and hurt me if I dozed off. I got up to check it seven times in one hour. I put my bo, my long fighting staff, under my pillow. I stashed the Whisper right at the side of the bed, where I had easy reach to it.

Teddy knew where I was now. He knew where I worked. My father was a yakuza mastermind. He'd overseen thousands of killings. Yoji Yukemura was presumably the same kind of man and had maybe even orchestrated Ohiko's death. And who was Teddy? I pressed my hand to my head in a desperate attempt to expel these characters from my brain.

Then I realised I'd forgotten the printouts again. I'd have to get them tomorrow. And I couldn't work at Life Bytes anymore. Teddy had found me in just one day.

The next morning I really needed the sunglasses. My eyes were puffy and red, with dark circles under them. I couldn't sleep, so I got up and went through some exercises on my own. Hiro was coming later; I had to go get those printouts from Life Bytes and talk to Farnsworth before Shigeto got there.

Taking the same route I had the night before was strange. I carried my bo with me, concealed in my coat. I came around the corner to Life Bytes, almost covering my eyes, afraid of what I'd see.

But Teddy was nowhere to be seen. I breathed a sigh of relief at the sight of Farnsworth unlocking the store. "Farnsworth!" I called. He looked over eagerly.

"Hey, Heaven," he said, looking puzzled. "A-Are you on the schedule today?"

I shook my head. "No, but I need to talk to you about something." I looked around me for any suspicious figures lurking. "Let's go inside."

As soon as Farnsworth got the door open, I rushed past him straight to the printer. All of my printouts were still there. I grabbed them and stuffed them into my coat. "Listen," I said. "I don't have much time. I can't work here. I have to quit."

Farnsworth looked like someone had told him he'd been diagnosed with a terrible, incurable disease. "You're kidding," he said. He looked almost like he was going to cry.

I shook my head.

"What's going on? Why do you have to quit?" Farnsworth said.

I bit my lip and looked around. I had this paranoid fear that Teddy was going to break in any minute and catch me off guard. "I can't explain," I whispered.

"You're acting so strange . . . ," Farnsworth said.

I shook my head again, my eyes filling with tears.

Farnsworth shyly shifted from one foot to the other, tentatively putting his hand on my shoulder. He said. "It's okay. It's okay, Heaven. You don't have to explain. Do you need some help or anything? Is there anything I can . . . uh . . . do?"

I shook my head and tried to smile. "Thanks," I said. "I'm so sorry."

Farnsworth snorted. "Don't worry about it. We really didn't need somebody, anyway. But it was nice to have you here." He said that last part quietly, not looking me in the eye.

I glanced around again. "Look, I would love to stay and, uh, talk some more, but I should get out of here."

"Okay," Farnsworth said. Then he held up a finger. "Hold on. I have something for you. The Professor was able to get you something last night. He brought it by after you left." He went in the back office and came out with a paper bag. He pulled out three strange-looking cell phones. They were brown and looked like they were made out of cardboard and bits of cheap plastic. "Disposable cell phones," he said. "You use them a few times, then throw them away. He said if you need more, just give him a call."

"Thanks," I whispered. Then I had a terrible thought. What if Shigeto had overheard our conversation about the cell phones? Was there any way he had the numbers?

"Uh . . . ," I began, "do you know if anyone else knows about these? I mean, besides you and the Professor."

Farnsworth looked confused. "I don't think so," he said. "I mean, the Prof came by late last night, right before I closed up. Everyone was gone. Heaven . . ." He looked at me sadly. "Are you in some kind of trouble?" He raised his eyebrows curiously. I could feel how badly he wanted to help.

I forced myself to shake my head, anyway. "It's better if you don't know," I said, taking the bag and walking towards the door.

"If you need anything . . ." Farnsworth said again.

"I'll call you," I answered. I raised my hand in a wave.

"I'll talk to you soon," I said. Farnsworth gave me a sad smile. He still looked about ready to cry. I walked out the door.

I got back home without a hitch and put the bag of cell phones in my room. There was a message from Hiro on my machine: "Hey, Heaven. It's Hiro. We're meeting in downtown L.A. for practise today. Take the DASH and get off near Little Tokyo. It's on the corner of Los Angeles and Temple near the Japanese American National Museum. I'll see you soon."

Ugh. The *last* thing I wanted to do was practise. *Or* get on mass transit. And go near Little Tokyo. I didn't know what friends or associates of Teddy would be lurking around that part of the city. I had no idea *where* they'd be lurking. I put my coat back on and found my sunglasses on the table. All of a sudden I hated L.A. It was so huge and confusing. It was so difficult to get anywhere without a car.

When Hiro saw me walk into the warehouse, he gasped. "What happened to *you*?" he said. "You look . . . awful."

Oh, you probably say that to all the girls. "Great," I said. "I was wondering about that. Thanks."

But Hiro looked at me with kind eyes. "Heaven, what happened?"

I took in a breath, and my chest shook with tension. I needed to talk to someone. I felt myself break down. "I saw Teddy Yukemura in front of Life Bytes. I think he was trying to set me up. And I found out all this information about my father and the Yukemuras. All about the yakuza. Teddy found out where I worked because some guy from Life Bytes recognised me. This other guy told me my dad is a huge yakuza kingpin and I think my father has killed like thousands of people, and I feel like such a stupid naive little kid because I'd always *suspected* he was involved in *something*, but I didn't know what, and apparently all these things have been going on before my eyes for . . . well . . . my whole life and—"

"Wait a minute," Hiro said. "Stop. Slow down." He held me by the shoulders, the same as Teddy had but in a much gentler, reassuring way. "Teddy was outside your work?"

I nodded, looking out the window. I didn't want to meet Hiro's eyes. Seeing pity there would only make it worse.

"And he found you because some guy came in and recognised you and told Teddy. But how did the guy recognise you?"

I sighed. "He saw me looking up information on the Internet about my father."

Hiro stared at me. He shook his head, as if he hadn't heard me correctly. "Why did you do that?"

"Because I wanted to see what I could find out about my father. I thought I might learn something about who might be after me. And I did. My father is a yakuza boss, Hiro. Someone from his crew may have double-crossed him, or someone from the Yukemuras may be after me. They're a rival family."

Hiro sighed. "A crucial strategy that I've been trying to get through to you in training is knowing your enemy and not revealing yourself. I know that you wanted to find things out that could help you and your father, but it wasn't wise to look for information in a place where you didn't know who surrounded you. Especially information that could give away your identity."

"I know," I said quietly, staring at the ground. I noticed Hiro didn't seem very shocked to learn that my father was a kingpin of the yakuza. Had he already known? Had he assumed that I'd known, too? I felt so stupid, like the only person who hadn't caught on. "I'm sorry," I said.

Hiro shook his head. "No matter. It's done now. But I wish you'd told me sooner than you did. Why didn't you call last night? You don't have to go through this alone."

I shrugged and immediately felt even dumber. I hadn't wanted to call Hiro because, in a way, I didn't want to interrupt his time with Karen. Or more to the point, I didn't want to *know* I was interrupting his time with Karen. If I hadn't been so brazen in trying to find my information, Teddy might not have found me. Or at least not as fast.

"Are you okay to practise?" Hiro said.

"Yes," I said, sluggishly straightening up. "It'll help me burn off some tension."

We began with aikido, making short arm punches to warm up. I could barely do ten. Then we added in feet, jumping from stance to stance. I was a half step off the whole way. We started the sparring part of the day, practising some of the defense moves I'd learned the other day. Hiro asked me to do a flipping move on him – the same one that I'd managed to do on Teddy. I took Hiro by the shoulders and planted my feet but couldn't get him off the ground. I was too weak.

Hiro stood back and brushed his hands together. "You're not focused today," he said. "I think what you need is to get some sleep. Let's end practise early."

I sat down on the dingy floor of the warehouse and stared into space. "I wonder if it's the Yukemuras who are planning all these attacks," I said. I shared with Hiro what Yoshitomo had said about the Yukemuras – that they were in pretty dangerous waters. I also explained that since Yoshitomo had told me about the Yukemuras, Teddy was probably involved, too. "If he is, it could make sense that they wanted my father out of the picture," I said. "And maybe they planned a kind of double cross at the wedding."

"There are definitely things we should look into," Hiro said. "First off, we need to see if Teddy is an initiated member of the yakuza. If he's working with his father. That could explain why Teddy's searching for you."

"That could also explain why I was supposed to marry him," I said wryly. "Well, in a way, anyhow." Imagine me, a yakuza wife.

"I know some people who might know if Teddy's in," Hiro said. "I have a friend who sometimes trains at the dojo whose uncle is in one of the yakuza gumi. He knows a bunch of people who are involved, and I bet that if Yukemura's the oyabun, then it's pretty common knowledge if Yukemura's son is in, too. Let me go make some calls to find out." He walked to the far end of the room, where a phone hung from the wall.

I stared out of the dingy windows. I was so exhausted, I could hardly keep myself in a sitting position. It was nice that Hiro was paying all this attention to me. Maybe . . . ?

I frowned to myself. *Distance, Heaven,* I told myself. I had to get over him. I lay down on the mat and went into a very brief, light sleep.

Hiro tapped me on the shoulder with his foot. "Heaven, wake up."

I opened my eyes. Hiro stood over me, looking serious. For one brief, ridiculous moment I flashed back to the kissing part of my dream. What if I just leaned up into him . . . cupped his cheek in my hand . . .

"My friend had a lot to say," he said. "First off, Teddy is definitely an initiated member of the yakuza. He was initiated sometime last year. He was given a tattoo of initiation."

I remembered seeing the tattoo on Teddy's arm last night. Why hadn't I noticed it before? Well, probably because I hadn't spent much time with Teddy, and most of the times we'd had together weren't too up close and personal. Tattoos in Japan indicated an initiated yakuza member. It was frowned upon to get a tattoo if you weren't connected, so it was funny to see all these people in the States with tons of tattoos all over their bodies.

"The Yukemura family are schooled in martial street arts and aren't above torturing their victims. Their business is very different than the Kogo family's," Hiro said. "Yoji is rumoured to have a huge interest in drugs. He's trying to bring the Yukemura family into the drug trade."

"I don't understand why they wanted to marry us," I said

with a frown. "If their businesses are so different, I mean. Why would my father choose the Yukemuras, of all the families he had to choose from?"

Hiro shook his head. "I don't know," he said. "But stay away from Teddy until we can find out more."

I agreed and stared out the window at the downtown L.A. streets. The smog was so thick that you could hardly see a foot in front of you. It looked ominous, like death waited close, somewhere on the horizon.

My room is pitch-black. Smoke from last night's party still smells terrible. It lingers. I can't bear to open my eyes, but Gojo out there is making some noise.

I roll out of bed. Bagel. I stick it in the toaster and stand, still sorta messed up from last night, staring. My kitchen looks like a bomb went off. What were those dudes doing after I went to sleep? Who the hell knows.

I was dreaming about my dad. He was saying, Get it done. You're not safe. I know I'm not safe, Chief. Settle down. Japan is the only place you're safe, he said in the dream.

Get it done, he said.

It will mean big money.

This is your biggest move.

The biggest move for our family.

Can you help me? I asked.

He didn't answer.

He gives me bodyguards. I get to push them around. It's a good feeling. I get to make sure they get me what I need . . . a rock of this, a spliff of that, whatever. It's all here, and I am the king of the house.

I love the power. And I have a plan.

I shuffle into the living room and sit down with my breakfast. Gojo is watching TV. "What is this crap you're watching?" I say.

"You want me to change it?" Gojo says. He's terrified of me, I swear to God. What year was he born? Year of the Ostrich?

I shake my head and grunt. I think back to my conversation with my father. I am oyabun; you are kobun, he told me. You do what I need you to do. You are under my control.

Not for long, though.

Then there's Heaven.

Outside that coffee shop, whoa. Never really talked to her much. Was looking forward to having her as my wife, you know, in that way that a woman is supposed to be your wife. I thought I'd probably, I don't know, have tons of other girls everywhere I went. I've seen my father work a room. It comes with the business.

But last night was something else.

I never imagined Heaven, like, independent and stuff, but it suits her. I'd always thought she was a spoiled, quiet, surly rich girl who wouldn't say a word unless Daddy told her she could speak. But seeing her last night – she was a regular badass. Now . . . flipping me, acting all tough, her body this . . . this sexy machine now! I like this Heaven better than the society princess. She was such a tightass back then.

But still, I need her. I should probably get a move on before it gets too late.

"Your father called for you again," Gojo says, all timid like a pussycat. "He wants you to call him back as soon as possible." Gojo is terrified of my father.

Then I realise: The conversation I had with my father in my sleep – I wasn't dreaming. This was a conversation I had with him last night.

I shake my head and take a gigantic bite of my bagel. My father, when all this is over, won't even know what hit him. "All in good time, my good man," I say, slapping Gojo on his thigh. He jumps. "All in good time."

Teddy

109

9

I sat on my little bed and watched yet another hour of soap operas. I had watched so many soap operas in the past few days, the crazy plots were beginning to seem normal to me. For a few brief seconds the night before, I had seriously wondered whether Yoji Yukemura was planning to bury me alive. I'd even developed a plan of action, which in essence said that if Yoji Yukemura asked me to lie down in a coffin, I'd say no.

Cheryl popped her head in the room. "You want any microwave popcorn?" she asked. I wondered if she thought it was strange that I hadn't changed out of my pyjamas in the last seventy-two hours. Perhaps. Perhaps not. Really, who was she to judge my lifestyle choice?

I shook my head. "Nah," I said. I was pretty sure there was still some popcorn somewhere in my pyjamas from the day before. I glanced at the magazines lying on the ground. Which one did I want to read next? I leaned over and the magazines that had been resting on my stomach all slid off onto the floor. I lay there for a few moments, upside down, suspended, too lazy to even pull myself back up. I didn't know what I wanted to do next.

It had been four days since the incident with Teddy. Ever since then I'd been too petrified to leave the house. After Hiro escorted me home, I slept a dreamless sleep. I had horrible fears of being attacked in the middle of the night. I scoured the Internet printouts from Life Bytes for any clues I might have missed about yakuza, my father, or Yoji Yukemura. Cheryl's old roommate had owned the computer and had taken it with him, so I was out of luck if I wanted to go online now. I had to use the info I'd already gathered. Naturally I was dying to look up stuff on Teddy. I could have gone to the Echo Park branch of the L.A. library, but I was too scared. My research would have to wait.

Mostly I'd been spending the last few days just staring at the wall, too frozen to do anything at all. I hadn't even dreamed of looking for another job, although Hiro had suggested it might be a good idea. Money would become an issue. I only had a few hundred dollars to my name, and it would be rent time before I knew it. I was screwed.

I listened to the lulling sound of Cheryl's popcorn maker and closed my eyes. Suddenly I saw Teddy in front of me. He was huge and hulking and wearing only little boxer shorts. His ropy muscles rippled and danced, ready to tear me apart. He was *covered* in tattoos. "It's time, Heaven," he said. He spoke in a low voice like Hannibal Lecter in *Silence of the Lambs*. "Your father can't take care of you anymore. I'm here for you now." He began seductively crawling towards me on the bed. He took my foot in his hand and began to slowly caress it, using soft but sure movements. Then his hand ran up my ankle, to my calf, towards my knee.

I slithered off the bed to the corner of the room. "What do you want?" I said. "Go away."

Teddy laughed and pulled out a giant pill. It was the colour of jade. "Here, take this," he said. "It will make you forget everything." His arms and legs slowly turned into tentacles.

I screamed and woke up.

Sweat covered my head and arms and back. Cheryl poked her head in my door. "The phone's for you," she said. She took a look at me; she must have heard me shrieking. "Are you all right?" she asked.

"Yes," I gasped. "Bad dream." Cheryl handed me the phone. My heart pounded. What if it was Teddy? I looked back at Cheryl. "Who is it?" I whispered.

Cheryl shrugged. "Some girl," she said. "She didn't say."

Oh. Okay. Not Teddy. "Hello?" I said.

Karen's voice came on the line, rushed but trying to remain calm. "Heaven, it's Karen. Can you get over to Hiro's? There's been an accident."

An accident! "Is he okay?" I whispered.

Karen spoke evenly. "Yes, he'll be fine. But he says he wants to talk to you."

"I'll be right there," I said. My nerves stood on end. What could have happened to him? Thank God he was all right! I took extra precaution leaving the house. I put all my hair into a hat I found at the top of Cheryl's closet. I added sunglasses and Hiro's jacket.

"Bye," Cheryl called on the way out. She sounded a little confused — probably wondering why the hell I was so on edge and in such a hurry — but I didn't have time to explain. Even if I'd had the time, I couldn't tell her the truth.

Something about Karen's voice had disturbed me. If Hiro was okay, why did she want me to trek the whole way over there? I wondered if Hiro had been attacked again. A horrible sinking feeling grew in the pit of my stomach.

I made it to Hollywood in record time, zigging and zagging to Hiro's house. It was the first time I'd been back in almost a week. I remembered when I'd left: our strange, awkward dance at the door, my fear of making it alone in the world. Of course, I still had that fear. But I hadn't imagined that the first time I would be back at Hiro's house would be to see how badly someone had hurt him. My heart ached. My greatest fear was to see Hiro hurt because of me. Now it seemed to be coming true.

I felt a heaviness in the air. I was sure someone must be lurking behind a bush or a tree, but I cased the area before going in. No one.

I pushed open the door, out of breath. Hiro lay in the middle of the room on his back. For a moment, all I saw was blood.

Oh God, no. I thought I was going to pass out. Hiro was bleeding to death.

Then I refocused and blinked, walking into the room. Karen stood next to Hiro, poking around. When she saw me, she rushed over. "Hey," she said. She gave me kind of an awkward look. I realised I hadn't really spoken to her since I'd abruptly split from her apartment. Now that Hiro and I were training at other locations besides the dojo, I never ran into her anymore. She looked like she was searching for an explanation as to what was going on.

I looked down at Hiro and felt a rush of relief. He wasn't bleeding to death; his head was wrapped in a red towel. Clearly a steady diet of daytime TV was making me insane. *Maybe I should start watching CNN.*

Hiro's eye was purple and swollen shut. There was a little blood around his mouth. He saw me and smiled weakly. "Hey, Heaven," he said.

"What happened?"

Karen bustled into the kitchen and reappeared moments later. She ran up to Hiro with some kind of ointment and started to dab at his eye. "Infused comfrey oil," she said. "This should make the swelling go down."

Hiro winced; the strong-smelling oil must have stung. "Teddy found me."

"Teddy!" I gasped. "What do you mean?"

"Who's Teddy?" Karen asked.

I gave Hiro a wary look.

Hiro looked at her and then at me. "Karen, would you mind excusing us for a minute? This is something I need to talk to Heaven about alone."

Karen looked a little cautiously at Hiro, then at me. She screwed the cap back on the salve and brushed her hands on her jeans. "Sure," she said breezily. "In fact, I was thinking about going for a run." God, she was so adult. If I were in her situation, I would probably have thrown a fit. Goes to show you why Hiro was going out with her, I guess.

"Sorry," I said, and made a sympathetic face.

Karen smiled tightly, then went into the other room and quickly changed into running tights. She had an amazing body. She found her running shoes in the front room and tied them on. "Sorry about this," I said again.

"Don't worry about it," she said. "I know you guys have some stuff going on. You want me to pick up anything for lunch?"

"No, thanks," I said. "I'm fine." Truth was, I hadn't eaten in who knew how long. The thought of food made me queasy.

"Hiro, do you know where my blue running shirt is?" she asked.

Hiro pointed to his bedroom while still in the prone position. "In there," he said.

I wrinkled my nose. Even in the crisis at hand, I couldn't help thinking, *She's keeping stuff at his house! What's next?*

I scowled. *Stop it, Heaven.*

Karen closed the door, smiling sweetly at both of us. I turned back to Hiro. "I am so sorry," I said. "What did Teddy do to you? How did it happen?"

Hiro waved his hands for me to stop talking. "Don't worry about it. I'm fine. I actually found out some amazing stuff."

"But your eye . . . ," I started.

Hiro shook his head. "It doesn't really hurt. But listen. Teddy Yukemura tracked me down while I was on my bike earlier today for work. He was all puffed up about it, said he'd been following me for a while before he actually was able to tackle me."

"How did you know it was him?" I asked. I tried to remember if Hiro had ever met Teddy. I didn't think so.

Hiro laughed. "He told me his name outright. And he fit your description. Thuggish, tall, hunched, looks ready to beat someone up. Dyed blond, slicked hair, sort of smart-looking beady little eyes. Anyway, I was coming around this sort of dead-end street corner, and all of a sudden this guy comes lunging at me and pushes me down."

"Oh my God," I said. This was all my fault. I put my head in my hands.

"Heaven. Pull yourself together," Hiro said. "I'm fine. Let me finish my story. Teddy got in a couple of good punches, but I was able to get him into a headlock. After that, I was able to find out some interesting stuff."

"Really?" I said, sort of excited, sort of nervous. "What?"

"First off, Teddy has done some thorough searching for you. He thought about where you might go in L.A. and then canvassed Ohiko's friends in the area that you might have sought out. He came up with only a few. I was one of them. He was pretty cocky about all this detective work, even while in a headlock."

"Not surprising," I muttered. Teddy seemed to be the cocky type.

"Anyway, he'd been following me for a while. Didn't find my neighbourhood but found what I looked like, traced me to my messenger job. Followed me all around the city; I guess he got a bike. Saw me go into a warehouse the other day in downtown L.A. Then saw *you* go into the same warehouse. Remember that day?"

I blinked, in shock. Teddy had been watching us.

"He added it up. We were hanging out together. He didn't know why. He wanted to know what we were doing together. He thought we were dating or something. That's the way he said it: 'What do you want with Heaven? Why are you taking her into warehouses? Is that where you get with her?' He was insanely jealous."

I thought about this for a second. "Wait. Teddy put two and two together on Sunday?" Sunday was the day we'd trained in the warehouse; Saturday was the day Teddy and I'd had our showdown in front of Life Bytes. It was Wednesday.

Hiro looked up at the ceiling. "That's right."

"Interesting," I said. "Does that mean that whoever staged the attacks on us – which were, when? About a week ago? Whoever that was couldn't have been Teddy. He didn't know where you lived at that point. He didn't know we were hanging out together."

"Maybe," Hiro said. "But who knows what kind of line he was feeding me? I mean, he could say anything. He says that he found me through my messenger job, but he might have found me long before that or through my address. Who knows? He could've had guys staked out around here looking for you and me together, just in case. I don't trust him for a minute. Anyway, the best part is what he said next," Hiro went on. "So he asks why we're hanging out. I say that I'm the one

117

asking the questions, not him. So then he says he intends to marry you, and no one can stop him."

I nearly screamed. "Marry me?" I said. "He still thinks he's going to *marry* me?"

"That's right," Hiro said. "He thinks I'm getting in the way. That's why he wanted to rough me up. He's dead set on marrying you. He also mumbled something about money. And his father. Like money he'll receive or something. He was pretty much ranting and raving at that point, so I couldn't make much sense of it. Then I knocked him out and took off."

I thought about this. "Teddy was going to receive money for marrying me," I said out loud. "That sounds likely. From what I know about the yakuza, anyway, usually every deal they do is for money. And that includes deals of marriage."

"Yeah, he was definitely saying something about money," Hiro said.

"And Teddy, well, Teddy loves money," I said. "Ohiko used to tell me stories about him back in Japan. Everyone knew that while he was in school, he was this big-time gambler. He set up a little casino, people said, in the back of his house. Not that Ohiko went or anything. The thing was totally crooked. But I thought it was just, you know, kids being stupid . . ." I trailed off. Teddy had *yakuza* written all over him, even as a kid. I was sure he was into drugs as well. Plus I remembered Ohiko talking about how Teddy was addicted to shoplifting from some of the high-fashion boutiques and record stores, even though he had more than enough money to pay for things. Teddy was made for a life of crime.

And if Teddy had money coming to him, he'd stop at nothing to get it. Which explained why he'd been looking for me at Life Bytes. If he needed to marry me, he'd need me alive. "Maybe he's not a threat," I said.

"Unless he's bluffing," Hiro said.

"Yeah, true. But this marriage scheme for money seems more like him. I'm glad you were around to 'get in the way,'" I said, laughing awkwardly at my own joke. God, if only Hiro were an actual threat to my singledom! I squared my shoulders. "Although, of course, I would have never wanted you to get beat up or anything . . ."

"Please," Hiro said, sitting up. "I just hope it helped some."

"Definitely," I said warily.

We stared at each other for a couple of seconds. I wondered what Hiro was thinking. What a mess I'd got him into. I felt a strange tingliness running over my body. Hiro had got beat up for me! He was helping me through this! I wanted to give him a big hug but wondered if that would be strange. I did it anyway. I threw my arms around him. He laughed a little shakily and put his arms lightly around me.

Hugging him felt pretty good.

We broke apart and I laughed. But Hiro kept staring at me with his one good eye. It was . . . it was completely magical. I thought again of my kissing dream. The tingly feeling inside turned up to high volume.

Then the door opened and Karen burst through. "Hey, guys," she said in a low voice, in case we were still talking.

We shot apart quickly. I'm not sure why exactly – I guess I

just felt guilty being that close to Hiro in Karen's presence.

"Hey," Hiro said, lying back down. "You're back a little early."

"Well, it started raining, so I just went and picked up some lunch. I'm sorry I'm back so soon. Is everything okay?" Karen asked. She walked over to Hiro and began stroking his hair. I immediately deflated.

Karen produced a couple of cartons of something steaming. "I picked you up some udon," she said to Hiro. "When was the last time you ate anything?"

"Thanks," Hiro said. "That's so thoughtful." He touched her hand and squeezed it. She gave him a little kiss. I pretended to be fascinated with the picture of Mount Fuji on Hiro's wall. I didn't know what to do with my hands.

Karen walked into the other room to get their lunch ready. I noticed that she hadn't said anything to me. Was she still mad that I left her apartment without saying anything? Was she upset that Hiro had to talk about something with me in private? Or did she feel like we were competing for Hiro's time now? I wondered what I could do to remedy the situation. But in a way, I didn't quite feel like remedying it. Hiro had needed to tell me something. I had a right to my privacy. If Karen knew anything, she could put herself in danger. But how to explain that to her without divulging any information? I hoped that Hiro was smart enough not to get her involved.

I turned to Hiro. "Well, I think I'm going to go now."

"Okay," Hiro said. My heart dropped. I'd thought Hiro might tell me not to, but to stay and take care of him. To hear more about his run-in with Teddy. But I guessed now that Karen was back, I wasn't necessary. I wondered how he'd explained the situation to her. A bike wreck? A stupid argument?

"What are you going to do about all this?" Hiro asked me, his voice quiet.

I tilted my head. "I don't know."

"Well, please don't do anything without talking to me about it first, okay? I think you should continue to lay low. We should try to get information out of Teddy, but we need to think of a safe way. We need to get him in a public place. And we need to be on guard at all times. Be careful when you're leaving here."

"I know," I said. Then I remembered something. "I still have your jacket," I said. "It's at home."

Hiro shifted position. "Oh, right."

I looked at his other jacket, the one I'd left him with, crumpled in the corner. It was covered in blood. He wouldn't be able to wear it again. "I'll bring it back tonight," I said.

"Oh, Heaven, you don't have to," Hiro started. A little part of me wondered whether he just wanted me out of his hair so he could have the whole evening with Karen. *So they can have crazy wild sex.* I felt my face flush bright red as that thought crept into my brain. I thought of Hiro's bedroom, where I had slept my first night at his house. It was nice. Clean and peaceful. It could definitely be romantic. *Stop it, Heaven!* I scolded myself. *Be a grown-up! You have to get a grip!*

"It's no problem," I said. "Your other jacket is a mess. I'll come back tonight and give it to you. Maybe around six or seven?"

"Call me from one of those cell phones you got," Hiro said. I nodded and shut the door. *All right, enough lovebirds for now*. I had bigger things to think about, anyway.

I was starting to hatch a plan about how to deal with Teddy. I didn't want to talk to Hiro about it because it was dangerous and I knew he would be against it. But I had faith in myself to pull it off. I really thought it could work.

As I stealthily walked home, I thought about my theories. Say the wedding really was a Yukemura-Kogo link for yakuza purposes. Maybe for money, maybe for business, who knew. So then . . . who had planned the wedding attack? It wasn't as if the ninja had been after my father or Yoji. Or even Teddy, for that matter. Honestly, he was after . . . me.

Had Teddy really not known about the attack at the wedding? He told me he hadn't. Maybe Teddy was lying. Why did he need to marry me immediately? Why did he need money so desperately if he was now a paid captain of the yakuza? It didn't add up. But maybe the marriage money was more than I was imagining. Like millions or billions. Or maybe he'd be paid out in drugs. He'd probably love to get his hands on some more. But that didn't make total sense, either. You could only smoke or snort or inject so much – I assumed.

"Why?" I whispered to myself.

It was strange: Part of me had really wanted to believe that the Yukemuras orchestrated the murder at my wedding. But that didn't make sense now. It seemed they needed me alive.

Or maybe it was a trap.

At home I decided to try to calm myself down by doing

some of Hiro's meditation exercises. I sat on the floor on my mat and adjusted my spine so that it was lined up correctly from my head to my coccyx. I put my hands on my knees and breathed in and out, thinking of only the word *calm*.

In and out, in and out. *Calm, calm, calm.*

My breathing was steady, refined. I felt vaporous. I felt light. But suddenly the image of Teddy floated into my mind. Teddy beating up Hiro. Teddy looking blank and frightened when that ninja dropped down from the ceiling at the wedding. My eyes popped open.

"I've got to find something out," I said to myself. "*Something. Anything.*"

My mind was clear enough, but I knew I must be crazy to think I could pull this plan off. Who did I think I was, Commando? Arnold Schwarzenegger? Those sexy girl spies in the James Bond movies? But it just felt *right*. My heart pounded as I stood up and walked over to my desk.

I opened the paper bag Farnsworth had given me and rummaged around at the bottom. I pulled out one of the traceless phones. I rifled through some things on my floor until I found the pair of jeans I was wearing when I'd seen Teddy. I pulled out the little piece of paper.

I took a look at the address and then at some bus maps. Different stops, different routes. Timetables. I stared at everything long and hard. My plan began to fall into place.

I dialled the traceless phone.

He picked up. "Hello?"

I quickly hung up. Good, he was home. I slid on my sweatshirt and dark glasses, stuffing a tanto, or dagger, into my pocket, and did some warm-up, psych-myself-up exercises. I did neck circles and a little running in place to try and get the jitters out of my head. I went through the steps I'd take and tried to think of pitfalls. I had to time the bus correctly. I had to get in and out quickly. *Okay. You can do this.* But my stomach still churned with apprehension.

Finally I crept into the night. I was heading to a fairly commercial neighbourhood on the other side of Hollywood, not too far from here. A bit of a walk, but I was feeling clearer, determined. I knew what I had to do. I was not about to get caught.

The house was easy enough to find. It was on Sixth Street, right next to the central bus route through downtown Los Angeles. It was a rambling, huge old thing, staked out by a couple of big beefy guys. Bodyguards. Human attack dogs. I could see the television flickering in the front room. I slowly made my way around the house, learning where the exits were. The back door led to a little yard that looked like you could cut through and get straight to Central Avenue. *Okay,* I thought. *This is it. Here I come.*

Concentrating with all my might, I managed to slip past the bouncer at the front door. He was reading the paper and paying no attention at all. The door was open; it didn't make a creak to get through. I used the stealthy footsteps Hiro and I had reviewed. *Keep your feet silent on the ground,* I remembered him saying. *You are light. You are soundless.*

I saw him, slumped in front of the television, wearing a T-shirt and sweatpants. I checked around to see if any weapons were within his reach. Nothing. And the sweatpants were pocketless. Good. I'd caught him completely off guard.

I put the tanto to his throat. He jumped but made no sound. "Don't move," I said, holding his arms down. The sharp blade dug into his skin a little. I was shaking inside but managed to stand up. "We're just going for a little bus ride," I said.

And so, with the tanto pressed to his neck, I guided Teddy Yukemura to the unguarded back door.

10

We walked quickly and quietly to the curb. I disguised the tanto with my hand. No one was looking at us – yet.

A number-sixteen bus rolled up. I switched my position with the tanto and held it at Teddy's back instead. His back against mine felt powerful, terrifying. I couldn't imagine having the kind of bulk Teddy carried around. I tried not to think about it. I draped my jacket over the tanto so that it looked like I was just leisurely guiding him to the bus.

I dropped in two tokens for both of us. Teddy stopped dead at the bus driver. "Sit down," I urged him. "If you just talk to me, you'll be okay."

The bus was full of people. We managed to find a seat at the back. I'd taken the number-sixteen bus before; I knew that it took a long route up to Century City. If need be, the full bus ride would last almost an hour. But I worried. What if I finished my conversation in an area that I didn't know? I felt the pocket of my pants. I had money. I could take a cab if I had to, if I could find one. Otherwise I could take the subway back home; I knew where the stops were along this bus line. I was fine. I was strong. *Breathe, Heaven. Do this.*

"Let's get one thing straight," I said as we sat down, looking like two normal commuters. Teddy looked, actually, rather un-Teddylike. Usually he was decked out in Sean John or Ecko or Gucci or head-to-toe Nike, with souped-up-looking shoes and a lot of ridiculous gold jewellery – "bling bling," he called it. But tonight he looked like a regular musclehead guy riding the bus, not a spoiled rich kid who laughed like a hyena. I liked the way he looked better this way. He looked more honest. Not like so much of an ass.

I spoke in Japanese so the other bus riders wouldn't understand. An Asian woman sat up front who might know Japanese, but it seemed unlikely. Luckily, no one seemed to be paying attention. "I just want to find out a few things. So keep your voice down and let me ask my questions and then we'll go our separate ways."

Teddy frowned and looked straight ahead. I couldn't tell if he felt threatened by me or just inconvenienced. "You're something else," he said. Then he smiled and tried to put his arm around me. *Yuck. As if.* Maybe he was not sufficiently impressed. I dug the tanto into his back.

"Ow!" Teddy cried. "Watch it." He straightened up. "All *right*. What do you want to know?"

"Why are you following me? What do you want? Why do you still want to get married? And what was the plan for the attacks at wedding? Were the Kogos supposed to die?"

Teddy stared straight ahead. "Damn," he said through clenched teeth. "All right. I've been looking for you because I need us to go through with the wedding ceremony."

"Why?" I demanded.

He sighed. "To unite the two families, for strength and for business."

For the yakuza, I thought bitterly.

Teddy continued. "If you and I married, I would move into the second spot at Konishi Industries, next to your father." Right. This was nothing new. "The spot was meant to be Ohiko's. But he didn't want it. In a way, that was a blessing in disguise."

So I was right about Ohiko. "Why?" I asked gruffly.

"Well, because your father wanted to get involved in some of the businesses my father deals with."

Prostitution and drug running, I thought.

Teddy shifted a little in his seat. "Having me as the link was a great thing for the business. I could introduce your father to some of the . . . sectors . . . my father worked in. My father, in turn, wanted to be more involved in parts of your father's business. So each had a reason for the wedding."

Teddy sounded so textbook, so calm, so . . . legitimate. Then it hit me. He assumed that I had no idea about the yakuza. He was talking down to me just as my father did, trying to obscure the truth, to make everything sound innocent. I'd had enough of that! I glared at him. "Spare me," I said. "I know about the yakuza. I know what 'businesses' you're talking about. I'm not a child."

Teddy opened his mouth to reply, but nothing came out.

I continued. "I know about my father, too. I didn't know before, but I know now. Nothing is legitimate for any of you. When did you become a part of this life? Back in Tokyo? Would you ever have told me if we were married? And the wedding *was* a yakuza trade, right?"

Teddy sighed. "Yes," he said. He explained that he'd become part of the yakuza about a year ago. It was before the wedding plans had been made. His father had finally given the go-ahead for Teddy to join, to become the wakashu, or child, working not under his father directly, since he was the obayun to the whole clan, but with the saiko-komon, or one of Yoji's advisers. Eventually Teddy would be able to move up the ladder, become an adviser himself, if he proved himself and earned his father's trust. Teddy said that last part with a bit of disdain. He didn't exactly look eager to impress his father.

He explained how in the initiation ceremony he was given his tattoo. "I have a huge one on my back," he said. The tattoos were clan markings, a defiance of pain.

"What about Ohiko?" I asked.

Teddy stared straight ahead. "Ohiko did not want to be part of it. He betrayed your father that way. I don't really know what happened, but I guess Ohiko and your father discussed it, and Ohiko refused to join the business. So your father, who needed a successor to Kogo Industries, was presented with the idea of the marriage. That was what was decided."

Teddy cleared his throat. The bus stopped in a neighbourhood called Westlake and several people got off, including the

Asian woman up at the front. She looked at us strangely and stared at Teddy's tattoo snaking up his arm. I wonder if she understood.

The bus started rolling again and Teddy spoke. "The Yukemuras intend to go through with the wedding," he said. "We need you to comply."

I gulped. Teddy hadn't said, "Or else," but he might as well have.

But it still seemed really flimsy. Teddy hadn't told me about the money yet. From what he'd explained so far, it simply sounded like he needed to follow his father's instructions. "There's something else to this marriage," I said to him knowingly. Teddy shook his head, as if to say no, there wasn't. *"What?"* I said angrily, louder than I should have. Several people looked up.

"What?" I said again, more quietly.

Teddy sighed and twisted around a little. He didn't seem eager to show it, but I was pretty sure I was hurting him with the knife. "All right. Since you must know, I need the money for a business deal I'm doing."

"What is it?"

"It's just this big deal that I'm doing with some brothers in Colombia. Huge money. I'll be living large if this goes through. I just need some . . . well . . . up-front collateral in order to make it happen."

I looked at him, confused. I wasn't stupid – I knew he must be talking about drugs. I knew absolutely nothing about drugs and the drug trade. Talking about it made me feel seedy, as if I'd crawled into a different, dangerous dimension.

"This dude Angel contacted me a little while ago, right around when the wedding was happening," Teddy said. "Said he knew who I was and who my father was and what we did back in Japan and did I want to get involved in this drug deal. They needed some money to be kicked in and knew that we had it. So I said, Cool, let's do it, thinking my father would be all for it. I mean, money's money, right? Plus it was gonna be my money that I got from the wedding. Your father was going to award me about ten million for the marriage. Kind of like a signing bonus into Kogo Industries."

I felt nauseous. My father was paying Teddy to marry me, and Teddy was planning to use it to plan some massive drug deal. I thought about the elaborate parties that were thrown the month before we were married that gave Teddy and me a chance to "get to know" each other. They were lavish, over the top. The first one was my father's version of an "around the world" party. Each room was decorated like a different international city. In "New York," for example, also known as our ballroom, decorators hauled in two hundred pounds of dirt to create a mini–Central Park, complete with walking paths and a minicarousel. In my room they'd built a mini–Times Square with billboards and neon lights spelling out TADEKA AND HEAVEN YUKEMURA. My father even hired a Liza Minelli impersonator to sing show tunes on a makeshift stage. Across the hall decorators created a mini–Rio de Janeiro at Carnival time. Hired dancers danced the samba in huge, colourful, sparkling costumes. There were even mini–candy-coloured "floats" that drove around the room. It was like a whole parade, confined to one small space. There were four bands at this same party, each playing in a different room. There was every kind of food you could imagine or want, each cuisine appropriate to the setting of the room. The cream of the Tokyo crop attended. Teddy and I spent enough time together for photographers to snap photos of us. Then he ran back and wrestled with his friends, smoked cigarettes, did drugs, who knew what. I hung around Katie all night, miserable, wandering through New York, Rio, Paris, Beijing. I still couldn't believe I'd have to marry Teddy. The brief glimpses of Teddy talking all gangsta with his hands and making obviously lewd comments about the women dancers and God knew what else had made me more and more desperate. When we stood together for one of the photos, he said, in all seriousness, "You're going to cook me breakfast every morning, right?" I wondered if he remembered saying that. Things seemed so different now for both of us.

Teddy continued. "But then, well, you know what happened. We didn't get married. I still wanted my deal to go through. But my father said, Forget it, I'm not giving you any money. Finance the deal your own way. I want nothing to do with it. Unless you find Heaven. Find Heaven, and then I'll give you the money for the wedding."

Oh. So it *was* for the money.

Teddy was nearly trembling. "If I don't get this money, Heaven, it's pretty obvious what's going to happen. I'm going to get my ass kicked, that's one thing. They've already gone through with the job. It's my time to pay off. I'm running out of time, see? But if I do get the money, it could pay off for me down the road."

I stared at him. Although Teddy seemed a little grislier and darker than when we'd first had the pleasure of meeting, he was ultimately the same. A coward, selfish to the core. "So the big reason you need to marry me is so you don't have to stand up to your father," I said dully.

"No, it's—" he started.

"Teddy, please. That's why you've been stalking around lately, scaring me and my friends half to death, making me quit my job and nearly lose my mind? Because you're in some trouble with some stupid drug dealers and you're too much of a baby to explain that to your father?" I was boiling over with rage. "Baka. How stupid you are."

Teddy looked utterly amazed. I was sure he hadn't expected me to talk to him like that. "You should be a stronger person," I said to him.

"But Heaven, if you agreed to marry me, this deal would go through and life would be . . . life would be awesome! You'd have everything you wanted. You would be living the phat, plush life. *Bling bling!* Does that interest you at all?"

I thought for a moment. Of course it interested me. I was champing at the bit to get back to my four-hundred-thread-count Charisma sheets and my five-hundred-dollar Carlos Falchi boots. I was dying for a limousine driver again. Who wouldn't be? But could I imagine a life with Teddy? Could I?

"Do you know who attacked my father?" I said gruffly. I couldn't believe I was even considering Teddy's offer for a second. Who knew if any of this crap he'd just fed me was true?

But Teddy shook his head. "No, honestly, I don't. I told you that before. Do you believe anything I've said?"

I dropped my eyes. "I don't know," I answered. "Do you know anything about Ohiko? Who killed him? Who he was working for?"

Teddy shrugged. "I didn't know he was working for any-one else. I thought he was just opposed to joining the busi-ness. And I don't know who killed him. I don't know who that ninja was."

I looked back at him. Maybe I did believe something of what he was saying. He was very forthcoming with the details of the yakuza – braggy, almost. He was equally boastful about his deal makings with the Colombians, even if the deal was going sour. I doubted Teddy could make something up off the top of his head like that. And it explained why he'd been so pushy to marry me. It really did explain a lot. I didn't know. I felt pulled in too many directions. The bus whizzed forward.

"I have to get off the bus soon," I said. I knew the neigh-bourhood we were going through now. It was very near where Cheryl lived. "I don't want you to follow me. Get off at the last stop, in Century City." I'd memorised the bus route. Even if Teddy didn't get off at the last stop, I'd see that he didn't get off at mine, and the next stop was a ways down the road. "Okay?"

Teddy didn't answer. I knew he was upset that I hadn't said yes. He looked disappointed – almost sad.

"Look, Teddy. Please." I looked deeply into his eyes. Beyond the tough exterior they almost looked vulnerable, scared. Bewildered. "Teddy, if you are as innocent as I am, you'll want to keep me safe. And I don't know if I can be safe with you. I don't know if I can keep you safe. So please do this for me."

Teddy nodded. "Whatever," he said. "But Heaven, please consider it. Please. I don't know what happened at our wedding, and I don't know if it would happen again, but I didn't have anything to do with it. I suspect it has something to do with your father and your brother, end of story. It was something they needed to work out, but I don't know why except for what I've just told you. But I do know one thing, Heaven: I *can* keep you safe. I'm a pawn in this, too. We have to save each other. We have to help each other. I could really make you happy. I know it." He took my hand in his and sat a little bit closer to me.

I stared at him. I hadn't quite imagined these words coming from Teddy's mouth with such heartfelt emotion. "This is where I get off," I said awkwardly. "I'll see you."

'Think about it," Teddy said. "Please." He stared at me, his eyes growing large. The bus skidded to a halt and the back door opened. I stood up unsteadily, carrying the tanto close to my body. "Thank you," I said to Teddy. I backed away from him slowly and moved down the steps. He obediently didn't move. I could feel his eyes on me as I walked down the steps.

I stepped onto the concrete. I saw Teddy's slick hair poking up through the front window of the bus. He turned his head and met my gaze at the window. After that, I ran.

I didn't know whether to believe him or not. It was so strange. I didn't feel as disgusted with Teddy as I had before. Why was that? Today he seemed almost . . . human. Maybe because he had a knife wedged up against his back.

135

I made it to Wilshire but didn't see a cab anywhere. So I ducked down into the subway, quickly stepping on the train that had pulled in just as I rushed through the turnstile. I sank onto the hard plastic seat and put my head in my hands. My heart pounded. My head spun. The Yukemuras still wanted the wedding. Yoji was pushing for it to happen. Teddy would receive a billion dollars from my father. Teddy was being bribed by Yoji and in trouble with the Colombians. And I still knew nothing about who killed my brother and tried to kill my father. Only that Teddy Yukemura thought it was some sort of struggle between Konishi and Ohiko.

I stared out the window at the squat, dirty buildings of L.A. My world suddenly felt like a terrifying place, all its players darker and cruder than I'd ever imagined. I closed my eyes and tried to stop my hands from trembling.

Gojo calls me from a pay phone down the street. Is Tadeka with you? I ask. Put him on the phone.

Gojo says he's not there.

Where is he? I demand. Who are these people I have working for me? In the traditional sense, the kobun are to avenge the family to the death. They are to keep tabs on my every move with vigilance. They are to defend and protect me, as I do them. They are my children.

But these men should have their fingers cut off ten times over to ask my forgiveness. But no. Half of them don't even apologise. Instead they laugh. But then they see. Then they pay. It evens out.

I've been trying to call all day, I say.

I don't know, Gojo says. He was just here. Maybe he's gone to find the girl again.

What am I paying you for if you cannot even keep track of him? I say. Who knows what Takeda is doing in America. Sometimes I wonder if he is cut out for this business. It always seems like he's got something up his sleeve or that he's completely gone stupid or insane. Those people in South America: foreigners, others. He is blood, but he is weak. I've told him time and again it is the time to act, right now. Straighten yourself up.

When I was his age, I was already taken under the wing of Tenjunkai, who was then the oyabun. I was twenty-three and a common gambler street thug, disowned by my family, who were ashamed that I'd been arrested. One of my first jobs was working at the brothel and making sure things ran smoothly. I watched as the beautiful women walked back and forth, all

137

painted up. I was so mature, I did not touch them out of turn. Tenjunkai forbade me to. I was very obedient. He said that if I had, he would have cut off my head. Or better yet, he would have made me cut out my stomach: seppuku, ritual suicide.

But Takeda, with his gadgets and bleeps and noises coming from his body, with his swishy pants and his enormous jeans and his spiky hair, he is more concerned with image than business. His money will buy him more image. He will not be the one to take over Kogo Industries: I will. I fear Takeda's clumsy hand guiding the company into ruin. Now is the time, however. Konishi is seriously ill, powerless. There is no better time than now to get it done. And the wedding is the best way. And then I will tell Takeda that the empire he's been imagining is not as close as he once thought.

But I must wait. Tell him to call me as soon as he gets in, I say, staring out at the garden. And tell him not to leave the phone off the hook anymore! I slam down the phone and walk in circles anxiously, trying to push my visions of grandeur to the back of my mind.

Yoji

11

The one thing I was sure of after talking to Teddy was that I was hungry. Really, truly hungry for the first time in days. Maybe learning the truth about Teddy had settled my stomach. Fortunately, Cheryl had bought Krispy Kreme doughnuts. Their spongy sweetness was delectable. I ate three before I could stop myself, licking the sticky glaze from my fingers as Cheryl watched in disbelief.

"Hungry, huh?"

"Uh-huh," I huffed through a mouthful of doughnut. "Sorry. I'll buy more later."

The sugar wired me; I went into my bedroom and paced around in shocked disbelief over what I'd just done. *You're crazy, Heaven,* I thought. *You're crazy, you're crazy, you're crazy. He could have killed you. His bodyguards could have shot you. He could have screamed out and you'd have been arrested. Or . . . anything. This isn't some video game where you can just start again when it's GAME OVER. This isn't a* Charlie's Angels *movie set where you can just stroll off into your trailer once the shoot is done.*

I felt awfully morbid, mulling over what Teddy had said. My father had set up a trust of sorts for him to marry me. Teddy was involved with drugs and who knew what else. I wondered what kind of drugs. Teddy had looked like an overgrown dog sitting there on that bus seat. A foolish kid. I wondered what he really thought about all this. I took off my shoes and lay back on my bed. Hiro's jacket was draped over the bedpost. Then I remembered.

That stupid jacket. I'd promised Hiro I would return his jacket. But after the events of the day, I didn't quite feel like it.

But still, I'd said I would return it. I looked around at all the other things in my room that were his. I might as well give them *all* back. In my post-Teddy quiet hysteria, I shoved all of it in a plastic bag and came out of my room. I wore the jacket for the ride over, though. Just for one last time.

Cheryl sat in the living room, watching TV. "You leaving?" she said.

I nodded. "I have to go over to Hiro's to drop off some clothes."

Cheryl's eyes lit up. "Has he broken up with the girlfriend yet?"

I gave her a weary smile. "It's not like that," I said. "I'm not trying to break them up or anything." *I'm way too mature for that,* I thought. *Yeah, right.*

Cheryl winked. "I know. But you still like him, right?"

I shrugged. "Yeah," I said. And I still did. Way too much. Cheryl and I said goodbye.

I lugged the bag of clothes back on the bus down the familiar route to Hiro's house. I thought about how nice it would be to live there again as I studied the other people on the bus. Was anyone else having a secret conversation? I actually couldn't believe that I'd had such strange words with Teddy in a public place and no one had noticed. Goes to show you how observant people are.

As I walked down Hiro's street, I felt a little on edge. Like I was being watched. I froze and looked around. Nothing. Maybe it was just a branch moving or a bird. The wind picked up and blew bits of trash around. I was probably just paranoid from the Teddy fiasco. Actually, it was good that I was on my way to Hiro's house. I could talk everything over with him, all the things Teddy and I had talked about. Hiro would probably gape in disbelief when I told him.

Hiro's door was open and the lights were on, so I just pushed the door open a crack. "Hello?" No answer. I realised I'd been too spaced out to call first. I opened the door completely. The room was aglow in soft light. The TV flickered.

Hiro and Karen were on the couch, kissing.

I looked away.

"Heaven!" Hiro said loudly. "W-Why didn't you call?"

Karen jumped up, smiling. She walked over to the TV. Their faces were beet red. So was mine. I noticed that Karen's tight T-shirt was rumpled, exposing her midriff. She pulled it down.

What *else* could traumatise me today? How many nightmarish experiences can someone *take*?

I quickly stripped off Hiro's jacket and threw it down along

141

with the plastic bag of the other clothes. "Just dropping off some stuff," I said, not making eye contact with either of them. "I'll go now."

"No!" Karen said quickly. "Honestly, I should go. It's late, it's cold. I should go." She looked so uncomfortable, I suddenly felt really bad. Karen hadn't done anything wrong except let Hiro fall for her. None of this was *her* fault.

"No, Karen, that's why you should stay," Hiro said. I noticed his bruised eye looked much better. The swelling had gone down significantly. "It's getting colder and darker outside, and . . . it could be dangerous out there. At . . . this hour. It's late."

It was only eight-thirty. But I knew what Hiro was getting at. *Now that Heaven's arrived, who knows who's lingering outside.* Crazy people. Crazy people who want to attack. Great. *I just trail ninjas and thugs wherever I go.*

"No, it's cool. I'll go. I have to get up really early tomorrow. Early class." Karen shot me an apologetic smile. God, after being here this morning, acting all secretive with Hiro, now I was back again, practically forcing her to leave. She probably thought I was such a bitch. But I wasn't able to explain myself. I couldn't.

"But Karen—" Hiro protested.

"No, don't worry about me," Karen said, putting on her shoes. "You guys stay."

"No, I'll go," I said. This was getting ridiculous. "Really, I just came by to drop off some stuff. I need to get some sleep. Here's your clothes, Hiro."

But Karen had her shoes on. "Really, Heaven," she said. She grabbed Hiro's jacket, the one I took off. She smiled sweetly. "Do you mind if I wear this? It's kinda cold out there."

Hiro looked like he would have agreed to anything she suggested. "Sure," he said. I felt like I was going to cry.

"Bye, everyone!" Karen sang. How could she be so cheerful? "See you tomorrow! And Heaven, we should hang out soon. Okay?"

"Sure," I said distantly. I couldn't even wrap my brain around hanging out with Karen again. "That would be great."

Karen shut the door and left. I heard her footsteps skip happily down Hiro's front walk. A car's tires squealed outside.

I turned guiltily to Hiro. "Hey," I said. Hiro looked a little disappointed, but his good manners prevented him from seriously freaking out. *Not getting laid tonight, huh?* I thought, then instantly felt catty and stupid. Hiro wasn't like that. Even with Karen, I knew he could never be like that. I sat down on the chair nearest to the door. "So . . . I just met with Teddy."

That got his attention. He stared at me, not saying anything, waiting for me to explain.

"He doesn't want to kill me," I went on.

Hiro rubbed his temples. I could tell he was angry. "What possessed you to meet with him? You can't just call up Teddy and say, Hey, let's have coffee or a drink at the juice bar! He could be a killer, Heaven!"

"Whoa, settle down," I said gently. "It wasn't like that. I protected myself. I kidnapped him. I took him on a city bus and we talked. The bus was *full* of people. I had my tanto."

Hiro just stared at me, unable to say anything. I thought back over what I had said. All of a sudden the complete and utter riskiness of my attack hit me with resounding force. My stomach dropped out. My elaborate scheme now sounded like something a grade-schooler would think up.

Finally he spoke. "Let me get this straight. You *kidnapped* Teddy and took him on a bus. And then what?"

"We . . . we talked about everything. The marriage, what he knows, the yakuza, his own problems. He needs me. And then I got off at a stop and made Teddy stay on the bus."

"How did you *make* him stay on the bus when you got off?"

I stopped. "I . . . I . . . well, I told him to."

Hiro rolled his eyes. "Brilliant! And he didn't follow you home?"

"No!" I said, feeling my blood pressure rise. "Teddy didn't get off at my stop. And the bus's next stop was a while down the road. Then I jumped onto the subway and took it back to my house. It was dark. He couldn't have seen where I went. He doesn't know where I live. He didn't follow me. He didn't have any weapons on him or a cell phone or anything. He had a T-shirt and some ratty sweatpants with no pockets."

Hiro put his head in his hands. "Oh, Heaven," he said. His voice was muffled.

"I was able to slip by his bodyguards!" I said. I knew I was grasping at straws. "I was able to use the stealth break-in techniques we discussed! I thought you'd be proud of me!" As I said this, my voice broke and I realised how desperately I wanted Hiro to be proud of me. How I wanted him to feel *something* strong for me, something besides fear or annoyance. If I couldn't be the girl he loved, I could at least be his favourite student.

Hiro still had his eyes covered. "When I asked you what you were going to do about this, I figured you would – I don't know – you would *call* him or something. On those untraceable cell phones. Not . . . hijack him. Put yourself in danger. Teddy has bodyguards, Heaven. You just said it yourself. What do you think they're there for? To let Teddy get hurt? That was a stupid risk."

"Why?" I said. "I got what I needed to get from him. I *succeeded*. I showed that I can take care of myself." *Not that you really care. Not that anybody does.*

"All right, all right," Hiro said, a little more softly this time. "I'm sorry. I just . . . I don't know, Heaven. I guess I'm still trying to protect you. I commend the fact that you were able to utilise the stealth techniques. It wasn't particularly *ethical*, but that's okay. If you did what you had to do, that's great. I'm just glad you're all right."

I explained to Hiro what I had learned. He sat there listening with a disturbed look on his face.

"So it's definitely the Yukemuras who are out there looking for me," I said. "At least Teddy. I don't know if they want to kill me. Find me, yes. Use me as part of their scheme, whatever it is, yes. For Teddy, it's for the money. For his father – who knows? But I would guess they'd need me alive if they want to marry me to get control of Kogo Industries or something. I mean, that's what it would have to be, right? Marriage to get control of my father's company?"

145

"Maybe," Hiro said. "But I wouldn't trust Teddy completely. He's still a member of the yakuza."

"But if that's all you know and you grew up with it, how can you be anything else? Does that mean you don't have, like, the honesty gene or something?" I said. I couldn't believe I was defending Teddy. But then I thought of Ohiko. He'd grown up around the yakuza all his life and probably knew a lot more about what was going on than I did. And he'd wanted to go his own way. He would have, too.

Really, I hadn't learned that much at all. Maybe even nothing. What if Teddy had told me lies the whole time? Even with a tanto pressed to his back? Was it any worse than a tattoo gun? Probably not. I was glad there was no way that Teddy could have followed me home.

I sat down on the couch and sighed. Hiro sat down with me.

"Are you all right otherwise?" Hiro asked. He put the pillows back in their normal places on the couch. He and Karen must have knocked them off while they were making out. *Lovely.* "You've been a little strange lately. Distant. Like something's bothering you."

An A-plus to Hiro for figuring that out. "No, it's nothing," I said. "Just the shock of being here. And moving. And everything. That's all."

I swooned inside. Hiro sat so close to me. Close enough so that I could feel his breath. My heart literally *hurt*. I tried to shove the image of him and Karen kissing out of my head, but I couldn't. I felt like crying again.

"Heaven, if you ever need any help with something, you know you can come and talk to me," he said.

I nodded. But I knew that having me around was inconvenient to Hiro – and even, we now knew, truly dangerous.

"Are you still doing some invisibility exercises at home?" Hiro asked.

"Yeah," I said. "I've been trying to meditate, too."

"Good," Hiro said. "Meditation and focus are the keys to this. If you can master that, the skill will come to you faster. You will become a vapour."

I smiled weakly. My thoughts were anything but clear. They were probably more unclear, unfocused, undirectional than they'd ever been. Definitely since I landed in L.A. But it was nice to know that Hiro was still concerned about me, at least in some sense. I noticed he was staring at the couch sort of longingly, probably wishing Karen was back in that spot, lying there with him. I tried not to feel disappointed. Dangerous, sexy Yoshitomo had been interested in me. He'd found me sexy. I'd noticed guys checking me out on the street sometimes. But in Hiro's eyes, I was completely invisible.

Hiro came in covered in blood today. He said he'd fallen off his bike, but I knew. You don't fall off your bike and get a black eye. Someone has to hit you. I'm not stupid, Hiro. I work at the dojo, too. And then when he said something to Heaven about Teddy. Who is Teddy? But I played it cool.

After he came in all bloody, he said, "I need to talk to Heaven." So I got Heaven on the phone. Which made it even more painfully obvious that something was going on. Something that was getting Hiro hurt. And then he asked me to leave.

The more I think about it, the more upset I am. I hate not knowing. I hate not having some element of control.

Aikido is about control. Martial art is about control. Yoga is about control. Controlling your body. Feeling your body. Understanding. I thought that this relationship would be based on understanding, not secrets. But Hiro tells me nothing. And I'm afraid something's going to happen to him.

But I can't help being curious. I feel so close to Hiro.

I came over tonight and brought up the Teddy thing and he said that it was just private and left it at that. "I can't tell you, Karen," he said. "But don't worry. I'm okay. I'm safe."

We even got into a little argument about it. I said I felt insecure. How could I be left in the dark? Hiro apologised. He said that soon, very soon, he would tell me more. I shouldn't worry.

And then Heaven came back in. And I had to be happy and carefree and doo dee doo dee do, Karen is oblivious, even though it's not that way at all. And I said, Heaven, let's hang out, and she didn't even pay attention to me because she was so focused on Hiro and whatever big, important secret they're sharing.

I know it's wrong to resent Heaven. Clearly she's in some kind of bind. I just wish Hiro could tell me what it is. Here's this beautiful girl, closer to him than I even feel yet, and I can't ask why. Even though my feelings for him are so strong. Even though a tiny part of me is terrified – terrified – that there's more going on there than they let on.

I just need to sleep. I haven't been sleeping well at Hiro's – we stay up half the night talking, kissing. We can't help it. I snuggle into Hiro's coat. It smells a little bit like him. Delicious.

I hear a voice behind me. It's Hiro, calling out that I forgot something. I turn. There's just darkness.

Then I see a form, but I can't tell who it is. But before I can see, a hand falls over my eyes. "Wha?" I shout. "Don't say anything," a voice hisses. And then a hand clamps over my mouth, so I can't make any noise, can't even scream.

Karen

12

I was at a party. There were streamers everywhere, gigantic paper cranes, light-filled globes, tables full of mounds and mounds of sushi. I had never seen a mountain so tall with fish. Opulent curtains floated down in jades and scarlets. Women wore similar colours; I didn't see anyone I knew. There was a crowd of girls in the corner wearing L.A. clothes: tight jeans, floaty wrap shirts, funky sandals, toe rings.

I didn't know what the party was for. My father sat at a large table, a bunch of men around him. I recognised Yoji Yukemura instantly, even though I'd seen his face so few times. He sat at the opposite side of the room. Beautiful women surrounded him. Suddenly I realised he was naked from the waist up.

Teddy appeared from behind a screen, also naked from the waist up. He held a long hypodermic needle attached to a cord. A girl in a flowy veil followed him. Her face was powdered a ghostly white; she had on dark eye makeup that made her look dead. She carried a tray of what looked like watercolour paints.

"Hello, Heaven," Teddy said. I stood in the middle of the crowd of people. Everyone fell silent. The music came to an abrupt halt. My arms shivered. I opened my mouth to speak to Teddy, but nothing came out.

"I'm going to give you your tattoo now," Teddy said. "And then you will be part of the family. Your father can't help you anymore. You are one of us now."

"No!" I said. I looked frantically to my father but realised that he had gone. In his place was my old stuffed bunny, Bo. "Where has he gone?" I whispered. I swung my head back to Teddy. He loaded colour into the tattoo gun. He looked at me and smiled. "I'm so glad you've agreed," he said. "Now, this might hurt a little."

He moved closer and closer. I stared at him and backed away. "I don't want it," I said. "Get away from me." I had to get away. But my feet were stuck to the ground. I couldn't move anywhere. I couldn't move to strike him; I couldn't move to kick or block or anything. He advanced towards me, tattoo gun in hand, the crowd behind me laughing, happy.

"No!" I said.

I woke up. The clock was ticking loudly. How could I sleep with such a loud clock? I was sweating. I checked the time: seven-thirty.

It wasn't even safe for me to sleep anymore.

I realised that I should get up anyway; Hiro had advised me to wake up early today to practise some of my shinobi-iri meditation

151

before we met for training. He had to work this morning. I'd told him I thought he was nuts for wanting to go back to work when he got the crap kicked out of him the day before, but he'd insisted that it would be all right. Something about honour and duty. *Blah, blah, blah.* I put on my pyjama pants and slippers and slid down the bed onto my mat. I was in no mood to meditate. Or go back to sleep. I didn't know what I wanted to do.

The phone rang. And rang. I guessed Cheryl wasn't getting it, so I picked up my extension. "Hello?"

"Heaven. Are you awake?"

It was Hiro.

"Yes," I said. "Barely. I was going to meditate."

"Well, you can't this morning," Hiro said. "I'm afraid there's terrible news. Karen's been kidnapped."

"What?" I cried. I wondered if I was still dreaming. This seemed like a logical extension of the Teddy tattoo dream. I pinched myself. I was awake. My heart pounded.

"She's been kidnapped," Hiro repeated. "I received a phone call about a half hour ago. I didn't recognise the voice. But they said they had the wrong person. They wanted you."

"What are you talking about?" I said, still mystified.

"Look, last night? You came over? You came in wearing my jacket? Someone must have been outside casing the place. They saw you, remembered the jacket, and figured they'd grab you when you came back out. Then Karen came out in that jacket. She has dark hair, she's about the same height. They must have thought, That's her. And they took Karen."

Hiro relayed this information very solemnly. I could tell he was frightened. Last night. That jacket. *If only I'd left them alone – left as soon as I came in instead of shoving my way into Hiro's house so I could tell him my news about Teddy – none of this would have happened.* Or I would be the one kidnapped, not Karen. Would Hiro be this upset if it had been me?

"So what do we do now?" I asked.

Hiro took a deep breath. "Well, they said that I must trade you for Karen and she won't get hurt. I must come with only you, and they didn't tell me where. They wanted to make the exchange later tonight."

"Later tonight?" My heart pounded. And then what would happen to *me*?

"But I told them that you had gone away for the weekend and I didn't know where. I said you'd be back Sunday. I bought us three days so we can plan something. We need to start thinking. You've got to come over to the dojo right away."

"All right," I said, already putting some of my things in a bag. "Do you think Karen will be okay for three days? I mean, who do you think these people are?"

"I don't know." Hiro sounded like he was almost ready to cry – a startling emotion in his usually calm, controlled presence. "I don't know who they are. Who do *you* think they are?"

"Let's talk about it when I get over there," I said.

On my way over I was freaking out. My fears of making everyone's lives complicated had come true. Karen was now being held by . . . psychos, maybe, who wanted me instead. But who were they? Was it the Yukemuras, looking to kidnap me so they could get the marriage over and done with? Or was it someone else, some darker force that was even bigger than the Yukemuras? Even more dangerous?

It must be the Yukemuras. They have the motive. I had kidnapped Teddy yesterday; if he had anything to do with it, he'd probably shared the idea as if he'd come up with it himself. Although the mistaken identity was a strange twist. If Teddy had been the kidnapper, he would have taken one look at Karen and realised we were two totally different people. Karen and I don't look anything alike. Was Teddy sending someone out to do the work for him?

I got to the dojo safely. I hadn't been there in ages – since before my father was attacked. It looked the same, basically. I found Hiro in his office, staring at the wall.

"Hey," I said softly.

"Hey," he said. He looked terrible, like he was still in shock. "I think she was mad at me, a little," he said.

"Karen?"

"Yeah. We'd had a small argument. We made up by the time you got over, but there were things that were unspoken that I think needed to be discussed." He stood up and paced the room. "I guess that's why she left. She didn't want to deal with it at that moment. If we hadn't fought . . ."

"We'll get her back," I said, somewhat unsteadily. Two things about what he'd just said bothered me: First, if Karen hadn't been a little angry with Hiro, deep down, she wouldn't have been so eager to leave. Meaning I would have left instead, meaning I would be the one kidnapped right now. Of

154

course, that had been running through *my* head the whole way over here. But also, I realised Hiro and I had never discussed Karen: their budding relationship, his feelings towards her, what they talked about, anything. It was strange seeing this outpouring of emotion from him. It was obvious that he really cared for her.

"When I spoke with the kidnappers on the phone, they said they would call with the location an hour before we're supposed to meet." Hiro looked at me. "I told you they want me to exchange you for Karen."

He paused. "Heaven, how can I do that? I can't morally do something like that. I don't know who these people are. I don't want Karen hurt, but I don't want you hurt either."

I should have known I could trust Hiro, but it still really relieved me when he said that. "What are our options?" I asked. "Is there any way we could get both of us back? Like, plan an attack somehow?" They'd certainly attacked *us* enough, if it was indeed the same people.

"I don't know," Hiro said. "I think they would immediately get suspicious if you and I both came with big weapons and jumped out of the car to fight, or brought other people to help, or called the police. We don't know who we're dealing with, and we don't want Karen hurt."

I blurted, "Do you think Teddy is behind this?"

Hiro stared at me. "I don't know," he said.

"It makes sense," I went on. "He needs me for marriage. For money. For whatever. His father's in on it, too. Besides, I kidnapped him yesterday. He could have been angry or confused or vengeful and realised that there was no way I was going to go willingly, so he decided he needed to take matters in his own hands."

Hiro shrugged. "Maybe," he said. I could tell he was still thinking about Karen. "But even if it is Teddy, what does it matter? He's not going to own up to it. It's not like you could call him up and talk him out of it. 'Hi, Teddy, we've figured it out, now give Karen back.' Besides, if it was Teddy, wouldn't he know the difference between you and Karen?"

"Yeah, I thought of that," I said. "Maybe it's not Teddy. Maybe it's the Yukemuras and Teddy knows nothing. Or maybe it's someone else entirely."

"Maybe," Hiro said. "But Teddy does seem like a likely candidate."

"I could talk to him," I said. "He might give us the details of the exchange or something."

"No," Hiro said, waving his hands. "Don't do that. Don't do anything to endanger Karen's life. We've got to figure out another way." He wrung his hands together hopelessly.

Suddenly I thought of something. "Wait!" I said. "What if we drive to the exchange as planned in three days? You swap me and Karen. They start to take me wherever they're going to take me. And then when I'm alone with them, I take them down."

"Take them down?" Hiro said slowly. He shook his head. "No way, Heaven. You haven't been training long enough yet. You're not ready. What if ten men are there? Not a smart idea."

"But then after a while you could come back and back me up. It could be like a fake-out tactic. You pretend to drive away, I pretend to walk off with them. But once I walk off with them, I start my attack. And you don't really drive away. You only drive around the corner. And then you come back for me once they're not paying any attention. You surprise them from behind!"

Hiro shook his head again. "You watch too many movies," he said. "It'll never work. It's too dangerous for you. What if they have guns? What if they shoot you, and . . . that's it?"

"They won't shoot me," I said. "They need me alive."

"What if it's not the Yukemuras?" Hiro asked. "I mean, it seems likely, but are you willing to gamble your life on that bet? One of the essential codes of the samurai is to know your enemy. Shout into your enemy's mind, zen-kiai–jutsu. But you don't even know who your enemy *is*," Hiro argued.

I frowned. I just *knew* my way was our only chance. "But aren't all enemies the same? Aren't there principles to use against all of them? Didn't you teach me that?" I said. "Hiro, you have to trust me. I can do this. I'm confident." And I *did* feel confident. I felt full of purpose. I felt strong.

Hiro looked at me desperately. "I don't know . . . ," he said. "Something doesn't feel right. If I drove around the corner, I'd have to leave Karen alone again. Who knows where the exchange will be, or what she'll have gone through at that point." He sighed and stared at the ceiling. "Something feels weird."

"No, we have to do it," I said. "It feels right to me. And it's the only way we can both be saved." I felt calm and focused. I was ready to work. "They won't be looking for Karen after they have me. Besides, Karen is capable of driving her own car. Worst-case scenario, she drives away. We take the bus or a cab home or something. But that won't happen."

"How can you be so sure?" Hiro asked. He paced the room. I sat cross-legged, going over everything in my head. This felt like a good plan to me. After all, we'd pretty much run out of other options.

"All right," Hiro said finally, coming to the same realisation I had. "But it will take every moment of the next three days if we want to be ready. We need to learn scenarios with multiple attackers."

We got right to work, heading into one of the large practise rooms that was empty. We both knew, but didn't mention, that the practise room was empty because Karen, who usually taught a class in there, was missing.

We stood in the middle. I had never felt more eager to work. Hiro went through a few simple rules in a low, serious voice. "Don't telegraph your fighting style," he said first. "Whoever these guys are, they might know all sorts of martial arts. So don't stick to just one. Use everything we've worked on. Don't use exaggerated stances. Be graceful. Be slippery. And remember, whoever these guys are, they are not honourable. This is not like sparring in the dojo. This is dangerous. Anything goes. If you have to kick him in the crotch, do it. If you need to bite his hand or step on his foot or whatever, do it. Ordinarily I would not advise this. But this is not your normal enemy."

"I know," I said. And believe me, I *did*.

"Know your strengths and weaknesses," Hiro said. "For you, Heaven, one of your strengths is that you are small and you are quick. You can anticipate where people might move next. You have to use this to your advantage. You have to employ your stealth techniques, too. Even if these guys are bigger than you, they won't be able to get you if they can't see where you're moving around."

We went through an aikido practise called tai-jutsu – using different parts of your body to fight. The only thing I might be able to bring along with me as a weapon would be something like a small katana or a scarf, which I could use to wrap around the attacker's neck. But no Whisper of Death. Hiro explained how I could use my head as a battering ram. My shoulder to slam into a foe's body to unbalance him. An elbow to strike the chin. The wrist, when turned inward, to bludgeon the solar plexus. Even my thumb to strike his eyes and throat. My knees to blow into the legs. The ball of my foot for tense kicking.

"Remember," Hiro said, "these guys might not even know martial arts. They might get you in a hold or something. You have to know what parts of your body you can use to get out. And how to hurt them without using superfluous moves."

I learned the "crab" takedown: If someone pushed me down on the ground, I could push off with both hands firmly rooted on the ground and encircle the attacker's legs with my own, one leg in the front and one leg behind, basically tripping him and rolling him over on the ground. This move was next to impossible – it required every shred of my upper-body strength because I had to balance on my arms and whip my legs into the air to trip Hiro. But I remembered: I'd managed to flip Teddy only a few days ago. He was huge. If I could do that, I could take him down with my legs. I just had to *believe* I could do it.

We ran through some drills based on two, three, or four attackers. Hiro advised that I take down each quickly, either through tripping moves or blows to their chest or lower body, knocking them off balance. Then I should move to the next, and the next, and the next.

We rolled across the ground in stealth techniques. We dimmed the lights in one of the practise rooms and flew across the floor, running through drills of fighting and going in and out of invisibility. This was totally not what I wanted to be doing in a darkened room with Hiro, but I managed to get in a couple of blows using the invisibility. He stopped, panting. "You're actually getting the hang of this," he said.

Finally we sat down and meditated. Again Hiro said to think of the word *calm* and close my eyes. I did. But again I thought of random things. Airplanes crashing. Teddy and the tattoo. Ohiko hugging me in that dream. Karen, somewhere, perhaps in darkness, scared and alone. Did she know we were coming for her? Were they telling her anything? What would they do with me once they had me? What if I had to marry Teddy? Or worse, what if Hiro was right? What if these people weren't the Yukemuras at all?

What if another dark force was out there?

I was covered in sweat when we finished. "You did great today," Hiro said. "I know we haven't had really focused on practises lately, but it seems like you've really stayed in shape. I'm still nervous about the exchange, but I think if we work at it over the next couple of days and if I can get back to you as soon as possible that night, we should be okay."

I agreed. We decided that we would meet the next morning, early, for another full day of practise. I could barely walk home. Everything ached more than it ever had before. More even than when I started training in the first place. Now it felt real. Now it felt like I was doing something. It still astounded me that a couple of months ago, I had no idea how to do any of these moves. I had no conception of martial arts, of bushido. I had no idea how to defend myself, nor did I ever think I'd need to. And now look at me: I was whipping around the room, knocking Hiro down and holding my own.

It was so strange.

But as I walked home, I started to entertain my doubts and feel a little nervous. I could possibly be fighting five or six guys. What if it was more? Was I really prepared for this? What if they brought out a gun? What would I do then? Would that just be . . . it?

I couldn't let go of the nagging feeling that this was all my fault. I shouldn't have taken Teddy on that bus and forced those questions down his throat. If he'd found Hiro at his bike messenger job, of course he'd track Hiro to his house. How hard could that be? Of course Teddy would find out where Hiro lived and expect I'd show up there sooner or later.

I squeezed my eyes shut. *How could you be so stupid?* Hiro was totally right: Meeting Teddy on that bus hadn't been a good plan. It had led to a completely innocent person getting hurt. They were supposed to kidnap me, not Karen. I knew Hiro must resent that, too – at least a small part of him. If I had just *left them alone* like I should have last night, I would be gone and they would be together.

Of course that was what he was thinking. Now he must hate me for sure.

I can't believe these people that work for me. Insolence!
"Put me on the video conference," I say to Ojo. He is calling
almost a half hour later than our agreed-upon call time. Ojo
has figured out how to set up a very secure video conference
with an indestructible firewall. It is safer than using telephone
communication, most of the time. And because I am not near
them, it makes it easier to do our business.

Ojo connects it and I see the fuzzy images of him and Natsuro
in the boardroom. They are both wearing suits. It is very late in
L.A. I can see the city behind them, illuminated in the darkness.

They look solemn, like something has gone wrong. "What
is the matter?" I demand. "What happened?"

"We've made a mistake," Ojo says. "We got the wrong girl.
We didn't know until we got her back to the compound. But
she is not Heaven."

"What?" My blood boils. "How did this happen?"

"We don't know," Natsuro says. "It was a girl wearing the
coat Heaven was wearing when she went inside. It was an hon-
est mistake."

"That's no excuse!" I bellow. "There is no such thing as a
mistake!"

"We are correcting it now," Natsuro says.

"You must!" I say. "Do you realise how much money is at stake?
Use your heads, both of you! What the hell is wrong with you?"

Both of the men lower their heads in embarrassment. I flip the
picture off so I don't have to look at them. They are pathetic.

I stare at the blank screen. "Just make sure you can correct
the problem."

"Believe me, it was a mistake, and we will, and—" Ojo starts.

"I don't want excuses," I bark. "Just get it done."

They are trained for this kind of thing, and what have they done? How is it so impossible to tell one girl from another? Who do I have working for me? Idiots. I should have put them on the smuggling job back in Tokyo. The rice factory raids. Anything but this. This is my prize. This is the job where I need my top people. But who are my top people? Who can I trust anymore?

Yoji

13

I walked through my bedroom door and collapsed on my bed. My muscles began to seize up on me – I had no idea how I would do the same routine tomorrow and the next day. I sat on my bed, staring at a random spot on the wall. The exchange worried me more and more. How could we pull this off when we had no idea where it was going to take place? Our tactics would have to change wildly depending on whether the exchange was in the desert or the mountains or someone's house or a public place. I wasn't a strong enough fighter yet to anticipate and change my plan so quickly. I liked to think I was all badass, but the truth was, I really wasn't up to this yet.

There had to be an easier way. There had to be a way to find out what we were in for when making this exchange.

You could call Teddy. The thought popped up out of nowhere. As crazy as it sounded, I wondered what he would say. I remembered his words: "Heaven, I'm a pawn in this, too. We have to save each other. We have to help each other." I wondered how much of that was honesty and how much of it was just to get me to drop my guard.

Hiro had told me specifically not to contact Teddy. He said it wasn't likely to help – if Teddy was behind the kidnapping, it wasn't like he would just say, "You got me; here's Karen back." We had to go with what we had. Getting Teddy into this was too dangerous. Teddy was an unknown.

Too bad. I was going to do it. I was going to call him.

I went to my desk and found the little slip of paper with Teddy's phone number. I found a different untraceable cell phone and slowly punched in the numbers.

One ring, two.

Teddy picked up. His voice came out as a gruff grunt.

"It's Heaven," I said.

"Hey," he said, his voice sounding more alive, happy almost. My body filled with rage. How could he be *happy*? Was this just a day's work for him, kidnapping someone?

"So you got the wrong girl, huh?" I said angrily.

"What?" Teddy said.

"Kidnapping," I went on. "Does that jog your memory?"

"What are you talking about?" Teddy said. I could hear the TV in the background.

I was fuming. "Teddy. I know that you were trying to kidnap *me* and not that other girl. But you got *her* instead. I'm looking for answers. I thought you said we were both pawns in this. I thought you said we should help each other." I realised my fists were balled up with rage. I unclenched them and tried to calm myself down.

Teddy interrupted me. "Heaven, what are you talking about? Other girl? Kidnapping?"

"Yes!" I said. "Don't play dumb with me. I know it was you."

"Look," Teddy said, in an angry tone that made me a little bit apprehensive. "I don't know what you've detected, Sherlock, but I don't have anything to do with any *kidnapping*. Unless it was the little kidnapping ride you took *me* on yesterday."

"But then who? They took a girl who looks like me but realised it wasn't me. They want *me*. Isn't it for the wedding? Who else would want to kidnap me?"

Teddy grew quiet. I wondered why. Perhaps he was ready to admit he was holding Karen in the upstairs bedroom of his house.

"I don't know," he said. His voice came out broken, strained.

I couldn't believe this. "Are you saying you *aren't* involved?" I said. "You don't know anything of what's going on?"

"I . . . I don't," Teddy said. His bored tone was completely gone. He had become breathy, a little nervous.

I waited for a moment. "Where were you last night?" I demanded. "Quick."

"I was here," Teddy said. "The whole night. I was watching TV. I smoked a bunch and fell asleep."

A little too much information, I thought. "What did you watch?"

There was a pause. "I don't want to tell you," Teddy said in a small voice.

"*TELL ME.*" My voice roared. I was almost shocked I could talk that loud. There was a long pause.

"I watched a rerun of *Dawson's Creek*," Teddy said finally. "Honest to God. You happy now?"

I nearly burst out laughing, despite the task at hand. "You did?" I said. I couldn't imagine Teddy watching *Dawson's Creek*. I didn't even watch *Dawson's Creek*.

"Yes," Teddy said.

I quickly ran out to the front room and found yesterday's TV listings. *Dawson's Creek* really had been on the night before. Interesting.

"What *is* going on?" Teddy asked.

"I was over at my friend's house. Hiro. I went in wearing his jacket. His . . . um . . . girlfriend went out wearing his jacket. Someone kidnapped her, thinking it was me. They found out they had the wrong person and called Hiro. Who knows how they had his number. They must have been staking out the place for a while. They want to exchange her for me in three days."

"Where are you right now?" Teddy asked.

"I'm not in town," I said quickly. I still didn't trust that Teddy was telling the complete truth.

"Heaven, honestly, I don't know a thing about this. But . . . I want to help. What do you need to know?"

"You want to *help*?" Who was this I was talking to? A Teddy clone? Angel Teddy? Why on earth would he want to help?

"I . . . do," Teddy said. I could tell he wanted to say something else or was rolling something around in his head. There was a big pause, and then he spoke again. "Let me see what I can find out for you. At least where and when the exchange will be. Let me make some calls. There might be some things I can find out."

"Who are you going to ask?" I said. "You're not going to have them hurt her, are you?"

"I'll call you back," he said. Then he hung up.

I stared at the phone in my hand. What kind of bizarre universe had I stumbled into?

My mind swirled. Teddy knew nothing but possibly knew who to call to get answers. Or so he said. I realised, looking at the phone, that my hand was shaking. There was something about Teddy that freaked me out.

I sat down on my bed, waiting for the return phone call. I had no idea how long it would take. I wasn't in the mood to meditate. I did a few drills with the different parts of my body I could use as attack weapons. Strikes with my wrists and knees. I did some kicking tsuki karate punching techniques. Jodan tsuki, rising punch. Chudan tsuki, middle punch. Gedan tsuki, downward punch. Oi tsuki, lunge punch. Gyaku tsuki, reverse punch. Over and over I practised these. I got into a sort of subconscious, lolling rhythm. I repeated slowly to myself, *Keiko, keiko.* Practise.

I thought about Hiro at home. How lonely he must feel. How upset he was over the fact that Karen was missing. It had been a day now. Where was Karen? Was she sitting somewhere, terrified, a scarf over her mouth? Were they feeding her? Were they hurting her?

I was sure Hiro was disappointed in me that I'd allowed Teddy to find me. For not listening to him when I should have. For my ridiculous kidnapping stunt. What did that solve? So I knew Teddy was in the yakuza. Big deal. I had already deduced that by looking on the Internet.

169

But then I thought more about Teddy. Yes, he was scary. But there seemed to be a shred of honesty to him. He wanted to help. He seemed like he really wanted to tell me things. He seemed afraid himself. He had his own problems. I wished I knew whether I could really trust him or not.

My thoughts drifted back to Hiro. The emotions I felt for him hadn't subsided one bit – they actually felt stronger since I'd gone out on my own. But he'd found someone who was the girl of his dreams – who wasn't me. Hiro didn't see me at all. I was truly invisible to him.

That was probably why I felt so cocky about my mission. If my own sensei wasn't seeing me, then why would the rest of the world?

The detachable phone rang. I jumped. "Hello?" I said.

"Teddy."

I breathed in.

He spoke quickly. "The location of the exchange will be the corner of Winston and Los Angeles. Downtown L.A. It's going to go down in a garage at the far end of the lot. Eleven-fifteen. If it all goes according to plan, the girl won't be hurt. They only want you."

"Who does?" I demanded. "How did you find this out?"

Teddy sounded like he was speaking through clenched teeth. "They want you alive, all right? Don't make me tell you any more. They just want you so we can get married and the merger can happen. Then this will end. You won't be hurt."

"How do you know?" I said.

"Don't call me again," he said, and hung up.

With shaking hands I dialled his number again. But it just rang and rang and rang. He wasn't picking up.

I put the phone down, trembling. Teddy must have gotten this information from someone in the Yukemura clan. It *was* them. But . . .

If Teddy wanted to go through with this marriage just as much as his family did, why would he tell me about where the exchange was going to take place? He knew that we would probably devise a plan to escape. Meaning that the marriage would not happen.

Why would he tell me what he told me?

Unless it was a lie.

Maybe he made up the information. Why else would he call me back? But why did he call me back at all? My head hurt. I continued to dial his number, but no one answered. Was he honestly trying to help me? What did he have to gain?

She called.

I knew something was weird when my dad didn't call me all day. And then the next day, silence. What the hell was happening? I began to wonder if he was working on something else.

But then . . . yeah. I opened my blabbermouth, too, saying what we really needed to do was to kidnap Heaven because I thought that was the only way she'd agree to the marriage. I was halfjoking. I had no idea they were going to take my advice.

Ojo can't look me in the eye. "What's up, brotha?" I said. He ignored me. "HELLO?" I said, louder. Then the phone call. Aha. Ojo was in on it. And it was probably Ojo who got the wrong girl.

Who are these guys my dad hires? Idiots. How could they mistake Heaven for someone else? Heaven looks like . . . herself. There's no one else who looks like Heaven.

When she called and told me about it, I hung up and didn't know what to do. Marrying her would be the best plan. I knew it. Everyone knew it. Except her, of course. It would push all of my plans forward. Get those dudes off my back. Get my father . . . out. He'd be out. Whatever they had to do. That would be the first order of business.

But I felt compelled to help her. I felt compelled to do something for her, anything. As much as I wanted to be around her, I thought maybe this was not the best way. Not with my father in charge. And if I didn't help her now and Heaven was to marry me, she would hate me for life.

I don't know if I could deal with that.

Now I'm sitting here wondering what I'm going to tell her. I just spoke with Ojo. Pounded it out of him. He knew everything: what had happened, where the exchange was going to take place, what time. Now all I had to do was tell Heaven. Or not tell her.

Get a grip, man. Why the hell would I tell her? What is wrong with me? Am I going soft? What will happen to me if I do tell her? Surely they're gonna know it's me . . .

And the money. I need that money. But I need Heaven, too. I need her on my side.

I look at the phone. Call her and tell her the truth? Make something up? Stupid. Make something up. What are you thinking, man? Make something up. Wait, no. I'll tell her the truth. Yeah. It's better. No one knows she called me. No one will know that I'm the one who told her.

God. No. Tell her something, anything, but not what's true. They'll find out you told her! Plus she might like being married to me. Or she might hate it. Hate me. Love me. Hate me. Do I want Heaven to hate me? Make something up. Or not.

I pick up the phone and dial the number she gave me.

14

The following morning Hiro and I arranged to meet at another warehouse in downtown L.A. When I walked in to greet him, he was staring out the window blankly. He looked like he hadn't slept.

"How are you?" I asked.

Hiro shook his head.

"I called Teddy," I said nervously.

Hiro turned to me, a look of anger on his face. "Didn't we agree that you would *not* do that? Karen's life is at stake!"

"I know that," I said. "Believe me. But I had to see what Teddy knew. And if I'm judging correctly, he didn't know anything. Apparently these plans had been made without him. He offered to help. He called me back with the location of the exchange and the time when it will happen."

Hiro stood with his arms crossed in front of him. He looked seriously shaken. I felt foolish, too – every connection I'd made with Teddy had gone wrong before. Would this one, too?

"Where is it?" he finally said in a low voice.

"The corner of Winston and Los Angeles. A parking garage. Pretty close to here, I think. We can go check it out! And that means the Yukemuras are definitely behind this."

Hiro put his head in his hands and walked around in a circle. "How do we know he's not lying?" he said. "He could say anything. Melrose. The Chinese Theatre. He could have told us Englewood. Or . . . or San Francisco!" I could see he was getting a little hysterical. "Should we really go to this . . . parking garage? What if these people spring out and catch us in a trap? That's possible, Heaven – maybe Teddy set you up so they can just capture you here and now."

I shook my head. "I don't think Teddy told anyone that he was talking to me. It was very hard for him to tell me this information. I really think we could go check it out. It's a risk we have to take, but I think we should take it. If he's not lying, think of how I can use the space to my advantage! We could hide a katana there! Or two!"

Hiro paced and didn't make eye contact with me. "I don't know," he said. "You really trust him on this?"

"I can't say I trust him, but we have to go and check out the place," I said. "Weren't you talking about the powers of intuition that come with invisibility? Knowing where your enemy is? Doesn't that include knowing your enemy's battleground?"

"I'm more nervous about the fact that if we show up there early to check the place out, somehow they'll . . . know . . . and something will happen to Karen."

I shook my head again. "But I don't think Teddy told anyone. Why would they be watching the site if they think we don't know where it is? And . . . what if Karen is *there*? What if that's where they're holding her? We can get her back days sooner!"

Hiro scowled. "No," he said. "Let's just run through what we've got. I don't want to risk it."

I picked up my things. I had a feeling about this; I didn't want to let it go. "I'm going without you, then." I was tired of Hiro's way being the right way. I was tired of his endless lectures about things being done in "the samurai way." I was tired of Hiro not trusting my instincts. What if all this with Teddy was a hundred percent true? Then all of my tactics with him were completely right. Then my decisions would have been good ones.

I had to see what the place looked like. Hiro could rest on his haunches if he wanted – he wasn't the one who had to take the risk in there and battle who knew how many people once everyone else had left. I had to know what I was up against.

I stormed down the metal staircase outside the warehouse to the street. We were already on Los Angeles. I checked my L.A. street map and realised that Winston was only a few blocks up. Pivoting, I strode quickly down the street. My face crumpled into a scowl. I took giant steps and saw Winston looming in the distance.

Shoes pounded on the street behind me. I tensed up and turned. It was Hiro.

"Look," he said, a little out of breath. "I'd better go with you if you're insisting on going."

"Fine," I said frostily. I could tell Hiro was annoyed.

We walked in silence to the garage. It was a desolate, confusing part of downtown L.A. and would be even scarier at night.

We got to the address. The corner lot was a big parking area with a small garage with a metal door at the far end. The door was up; it was empty inside except for some metal folding chairs. No car was in sight. A few minutes went by with not a single person passing.

We stood watching, sensing.

"What do you think?" I said softly.

Hiro sniffed, as if he was trying to get a sense from the air. "It really looks like this place is dead. I don't see any cameras or wires or detection devices. If this is the place, it's just an ordinary, abandoned garage." He inspected the sidewalk, the chain-link fence enclosing the lot. There was no barbed wire at the top. "If we're going to check this out, we have to use all of the settings to our advantage. The street, the lot, the garage. Everything." He turned and checked out the escape routes to the street. "When I drop you off and collect Karen, I could drive around this corner and sit up the street a little; it looks like the view is completely obstructed. Plus it'll be so dead around here at night, it'll be easy to tell if they have people guarding the lot. You know, outside. Maybe they think we're gonna pull something like this."

"I don't know," I said. "But you better make sure the area's secure before you come back for me. We don't want Karen to get kidnapped again." It felt strange to say that – like I was admitting that I didn't matter as much to Hiro as Karen. Did I really believe that? What if it was true? Was I throwing myself to the dogs here?

Hiro frowned. "The important part of this operation is to recover both Karen *and* you. Not one or the other. I'll make sure it's safe, but don't think I'm not going to come to your aid."

I sighed. *Right*. Hiro's honour would never let him leave me alone . . . no matter how much he might want to.

We walked through the lot and ran through some scenarios on how we could use its surroundings to our advantage. Hiro strode across it to get a feel of how big it was. We went over where the streetlights were, which shadows I could use to duck in and out of.

Finally we went into the garage itself. It was dimly lit – full of shadows. The only light came from a lightbulb protruding from a wall. The garage was filled with nooks that would make perfect hiding places. I decided I would come back later and hide a katana there. Somewhere that I could find but the thugs couldn't. I would have to think carefully.

Hiro and I went through a few fighting scenarios in the garage. Again we discussed the shadows. "This whole wall will be dark," Hiro said. "By ducking back here, you'll be able to elude them. Your best bet would be to get one to chase you and rush to attack you but then slide into the shadows and cause the guy to attack another one of his cohorts. They would essentially knock each other out."

"That's a good idea," I agreed. I felt like I'd seen that in so many movies, but all slapsticky kinds of movies where the move would never work in real life. With real attackers – thugs hired to hurt, maim, and fight – was I capable of pulling it off? I wasn't sure.

"It's all about quickness," Hiro said. "And using the shadows to your advantage. Lure them to this corner. This is the corner that will work for you."

I decided I would hide the Whisper of Death in that corner.

We trained for a little while longer, keeping a formal, polite attitude around each other since both of us were still tense. "Do you think this is enough?" Hiro asked. "I want to go back to the warehouse. We're putting ourselves at risk."

True, the garage *was* a little creepy. But I was wired. Was this where it would go down? I couldn't quite believe it. What would happen in two days? I felt good, yeah. Honestly, I felt like a badass. But I had a feeling that these guys would be about triple my size. How had Ohiko dealt with this in sparring practise? He wasn't a big guy, but I saw some of the people he had to fight. Some of them were huge. And Ohiko had always come out the winner. What was his secret?

I agreed to leave with Hiro. We walked back to the warehouse. The air was eerily silent – which was strange, because even though downtown L.A. was anything but residential, it was the business district. Where was all the commerce, the hubbub of people who worked? It was as if the city were dead. It made me shiver and pull up my coat collar further.

*   *   *

I told Hiro at the end of the day that I planned to go back to the location the following day and hide two katanas, one being the Whisper of Death. "We'll probably be searched during the exchange," I explained. "Wouldn't it be good if we planted something?"

Hiro wasn't sure. "While it would be great if this really *were* the location, we still can't say for sure. What if it's not? What if we're doing all this work for nothing? Look what we've figured out today – I wasn't envisioning the attack would take place in a garage at all. Learning about all of those hanging hooks and the garage's strange shape was a gold mine. But who knows if it's true? Why should we risk losing two katanas if the exchange happens somewhere else?"

I frowned. Hiro still didn't believe me.

Still, I wanted to hide the katanas. And hide them I did. I woke up early the next morning and took the bus down to the fated location. It was strangely ghostly. A misty cloud surrounded it. I crept into the garage and found a very dark nook that was long enough for both of the swords. Holding my breath, I set them in, then stood back. I'd brought a flashlight; I shone it in to see if they were noticeable. They weren't. I reached my hand in; were they hard to get out? Nope. Easy.

I scurried out of the garage just in time to avoid a car coming around the bend to see me. I watched from behind the bushes as it passed; I couldn't see who was inside. *Probably no one,* I thought. Still, my heart was pounding at a thousand beats a minute.

Hiro and I met at the warehouse again. He was twirling around, doing a few punching moves, when I walked in. I went behind a wall to change into my gi. Hiro was really concentrating. You could tell he was nervous.

"I still don't know," he said later as we were taking a break, eating some rice and beans that he'd brought from home. "I just can't be sure about this location. We have to be able to adapt our plan. Why would Teddy just *give* you this information?"

It was honestly the same question that had been rolling around in my head. Why would Teddy tell me where the exchange would take place? He surely had some idea of my training and abilities – I would have had him on the ground in front of Life Bytes if it hadn't been for his knife. Or what if Teddy told them that we knew, and they brought guns? And would Teddy come along to the exchange as well, rounding up as many guys as he could so that we would be completely outnumbered?

But something told me Teddy's advice was real. And that he didn't have anything to do with it. But his motives had me puzzled. I knew he wanted to marry me. Couldn't he have just told us that the exchange would take place at Winston and Los Angeles, then when Hiro and I went to check it out, pounced on us and kidnapped me for good? I took a deep breath. It was actually incredible that Teddy hadn't been lurking around that old parking garage. He'd made a perfect setup for us, and we'd fallen right into it. The only missing link was that Teddy hadn't been there to claim his prize.

What was he up to?

Hiro and I went through a few fighting scenarios to adapt our plan. Hiro explained how to locate shadows quickly and direct the attacker towards them. He had me duck and roll and slide into a shadow in the warehouse about seven hundred times. My back began to ache after a while from so much movement.

During the training, it really felt like the old Hiro again. We were a team – working towards a goal. We spent so much time together over the next two days that all of my bitterness towards him melted away. I could see that Hiro really cared for Karen – the way he would look off into space sometimes, his seriousness about the operation, his nervousness whenever his cell phone would ring. I felt that he'd really found someone to love.

But still. I thought of that strange look we'd given each other the day Teddy beat Hiro up. What was that all about? The tension had been thick. Then Karen bounded in, and we flew apart. But we didn't have any reason to feel guilty – did we?

Suffice it to say, my brain was a swirl of activity, especially on the day of the exchange. We trained all afternoon, then meditated in the evening to prepare. I was back at Hiro's house again, alone, with Hiro. We sat on the floor and waited nervously for the phone to ring. The clock ticked past nine forty-five.

"Try to clear your mind," Hiro said.

I realised I was shaking, sitting on my little mat. This whole thing had me nervous. I couldn't help but imagine four sweaty, humungous guys lunging at me. Could little shadows really be the key to a victory? I read somewhere that sports stars envision their game before they play it to prepare. Marathon runners imagine running the whole race in order to win. I knew that I had to imagine coming out of the exchange alive and victorious – everything going to plan. If doubt crept into my head, I had to beat it out. I had to be positive. I had to be clear. I breathed in loudly. Breathed out.

The phone rang. We both jumped. I let out a little yelp.

Hiro raced to get it. "Hello," he said quickly.

He got a pen from his telephone stand and held it poised in midair. "Uh-huh," he said. He stared straight at me. A shiver went through my body. Was he getting the location? Was it completely different from what Teddy had said?

"Uh-huh," Hiro continued. "Yes. I know where that is." I noticed he wasn't writing anything down. Was it such a common place that he didn't need to take notes? "Okay," he continued. "Yes. We will be there." He hung up the phone and stared at me silently. The look on his face was stoic – I couldn't tell if things were good or bad.

"Well, what?" I said. I couldn't stand it anymore.

Hiro raised his eyebrows. The pen dropped to the pad. "You won't believe this," he said. "But Teddy might have actually told you the truth. We're meeting in a parking lot on the corner of Winston and Los Angeles. Eleven-fifteen."

I stared at him, feeling a lot of things. Surprised. Confused. Scared. A little smug that I'd been right. I checked my watch: ten-fifteen. We had an hour. If we'd have just learned this, we wouldn't have been able to plant the katana, practise the way we did, take into consideration the shadows, the light. "Why did he tell us the truth?" I whispered. Now I was even more nervous than before.

The hour fled quickly. Soon enough Hiro and I were driving to the location in Karen's car, which Hiro had found the keys to. The nervousness between us created a strange fog of tension. I wanted to joke about something to ease it a little but couldn't think of anything funny. I racked my brain. The only thing that came close was a joke Ohiko told me once, and I didn't feel like telling it. Nothing to do with Ohiko was funny anymore.

Suddenly I blurted, "So, what's up with you and Karen?" *Way to go, Heaven. Very suave. Because things weren't already awkward enough.*

Hiro perked up. "We're just getting to know each other right now."

"Yeah, she said something to me about it," I said. My heart sank a little further down in my chest. It was strange to talk about it with him. I'd figured if I didn't discuss it with him, it wouldn't be real. I mean, of course I *knew* that they had a relationship or at least the beginnings of one. Hiro's long face and nervous attitude over the last couple of days was a testament to how crazy for Karen he truly was. But see, he'd never said it outright. Meaning, I could pretend it wasn't real.

"We have a lot of things in common," Hiro went on. "I can't believe her strength. I just hope that she comes out of this okay."

184

"She will," I said. Somehow, even though Hiro was talking about another girl, the respect he had for her made me like him even more than I already did, if that was possible. Hiro went on to talk about a sort of random, mundane-sounding evening with Karen he'd had just a few days ago. How easy it was to talk to her. First I bristled – I didn't want to hear this – but then I relaxed. In a way, the conversation made me feel less anxious. Some of my awkwardness came from the fact that I really didn't want to hear about Karen around Hiro. But talking about it wasn't so bad at all because finally I was actually having a real conversation with Hiro – we'd had such stilted, curt talks lately. And we'd been so irritated with each other ever since I'd called Teddy. I felt relieved; things were slowly returning to normal.

We drove into the downtown section of L.A. It was completely dead down here – much worse than it ever was during the day. I took short, nervous breaths. It felt like I was driving to my own execution. I squeezed my eyes shut, and although I tried to put him out of my mind, I kept seeing Ohiko floating above me. Where was he now? What was he doing? According to the Shinto religion, after death every person becomes a kami, a supernatural being who continues to have a part in the life of the community, nation, and family. Good individuals become good and beneficial kamis; the bad become pernicious ones. Was that what was happening to Ohiko? Was he a good person – meaning he would become a good kami?

Yes. I thought he would.

There were some sects that believed in reincarnation as well. What if Ohiko were reincarnated as something?

How would I know it was him?

We turned onto the familiar street and rolled up to the familiar corner. I could see a car parked at the edge of the lot. I drew in my breath. The windows were tinted – was Karen in there? Was Teddy in the car, too? Another car was parked a little farther back, next to the garage. I could see the driver staring at us as Hiro slowed to a stop.

"Remember," Hiro whispered. "Keep a clear head. Do not let fear take over your mind. Keep calm, dash in quickly. Stall them. Wait for me. I'll come in as soon as I can."

I swallowed painfully. "Uh-huh," I said. One of the men was walking towards us. He motioned to Hiro to roll down the window. Hiro did.

The man stuck his large, round face in the window and looked right at me. I stared straight ahead. Hiro didn't say anything. Finally the man seemed satisfied. "All right," he said. "Pull in there." He motioned to the garage at the far end of the lot. The door was open.

The instructions given over the phone said that Hiro should pull into the garage, I should step out, Karen would quickly get into the back of our car, and then Hiro would back out quickly. The whole transaction, I knew, would happen mostly in darkness. I was sure they didn't want to do anything as stupid as give away their identities and allow Hiro to get a good view of who they were. The man who was flagging us over to the garage wore an enormous overcoat and one of those ski caps that camouflages your nose and mouth. Only his two round eyes poked through. I shivered.

Hiro steadily rolled into the garage. Only a thin stripe of light lit it from the inside. A car waited in there; I didn't know how many men were inside.

He touched my knee. I jumped. "Calm down," he whispered. "You can do this."

At that moment the door of the other car opened. In the dim light I could just make out Karen – blindfolded – tentatively struggling to get out of the car. Someone shoved her from the back and she stumbled, holding out her arms for something to grab onto. Ski mask man grabbed her and walked her over to our car. He opened my door.

Hiro made a little noise. Karen looked dirty and completely disoriented. My heart swam around in a circle. What if Hiro got so caught up with tending to Karen, he forgot about me? What kind of stupid plan had I got myself into?

"Step out," ski mask told me.

I didn't look at Hiro. *Centre yourself,* I thought. I felt my shoes step onto the cold ground. Ski mask guy led me away from the car and shoved Karen in, all in one movement. Holding my wrist, he said to Hiro, "Keep her blindfolded until you leave. Pull out now."

Hiro pressed his foot on the gas and backed out of the garage. Karen's mouth didn't move. I could see, though, that she was trembling a little. I wondered what she had been through in the past three days. Whatever it was, that was what waited for me if I wasn't able to fight my way out of this. I shivered. The headlights backed up farther and farther until they were at the edge of the lot.

Then ski mask guy walked over to the garage door, dragging me with him. With one swoop, he grabbed the top of the door and slid it closed.

It crashed angrily. Complete darkness surrounded us. No link to the outside. The door sounded heavy.

My eyes struggled to adjust to the startling darkness. That hadn't exactly been in our plans. I didn't know how many of them were in the room, but I could sense more than one. Only a small flickering light shone from the corner; I could see the outlines of more men in the distance.

This is it, I told myself. *This is* it.

15

Okay, Heaven. Settle down. You can do this.

Ski mask guy led me by the wrist farther into the garage. I snuck a peek to the door – it was shut tight. I wondered what Hiro was doing out there. Where had he driven? Was he talking to Karen? Was there a way for him to get in? Or was I on my own?

I turned my head forward again. My eyes had finally adjusted to the minimal light. At the back of the garage six men stood with their arms crossed. But no Teddy. There was a chair in the middle of them. One of them, in a quilted down vest, was smiling.

"Hello, Heaven Kogo," he said. "We've been waiting for you. We have some questions. And congratulations – we hear you'll be getting married." Beyond the chair I could see a small car with the door open. Did they expect me to go inside? And where was Teddy? I didn't see him anywhere. Did that mean he wasn't part of this . . . operation?

I didn't make a noise. I realised it was definitely the

Yukemura gumi that surrounded me. One of the men had an elaborate tattoo on his wrist and was missing a finger. I remembered him now from the engagement party with the city-themed rooms. I had been standing with Teddy as we were being photographed for the press, and he'd waited off to the side, ready to grab Teddy and go outside and probably get high or something. "She's quite a tasty morsel," he'd said as Teddy had walked over to him, looking me over inch by inch. "I bet she'll be a *tiger*." I scowled. I hadn't had to ask how he meant that.

Now, as he stared at me, his lips curled. His muscles pulsed. His legs looked like they could crush someone. His feet were made for kicking. I wondered if any of the men were carrying weapons.

I recognised another guy from the wedding – he had his hair slicked back and coiled in a long braid and had enormous hands. When I'd walked up the aisle, I'd fixated on him, thinking, *The people the Yukemuras invited are such freaks.*

Calm down, Heaven. I knew that if I dwelled on any of this too much, I wouldn't be able to go through with the plan Hiro and I had worked out. *Think positive. You are strong.*

I heard a small rattle from the garage door. Hiro! Was he trying to get in? The rattle sounded again. Could he be back so soon? Or was that just the wind? But even the sound of it lifted my spirits. I could do this. I had to stall them. I had to try.

Ski mask led me closer to the men. "Sit down," one said. "We just want to talk with you." My heart hammered so loudly, I was certain that all of them could hear it. The odour of cigars was stifling. I thought of Hiro outside, trying to lift the garage door.

Why did I not see Teddy among the bunch? I wondered what that could mean.

Ski mask shoved me into the chair. "Sit," he said. He shoved me so hard that I stumbled. My hand scraped against the hard concrete floor. Some of the men laughed. *Silly clumsy girl,* I knew they were thinking.

Do it now, I told myself. *Do it now.*

I snapped into action. I did a wrist roll to free myself, and I gave ski mask guy a solid kick to his stomach. It wasn't very strong, but he was so taken by surprise that he didn't have time to put up his defenses. I used my shoulder to hit his chest. He fell, slamming into the chair they wanted me to sit on.

I rushed over to the wall and felt around for the Whisper. The shadows were even deeper than those Hiro and I had practised in. I had memorised them. I knew them well. With the Whisper firmly in my hand, I twirled it around so they wouldn't be able to snatch it from my grasp.

The men stepped back when they saw the katana. "What the . . . ," the biggest one sputtered. I guessed Teddy hadn't told them that I might try an attack. Amazing. My brain stopped on this for a moment: Why hadn't he? Was it a trick? But I quickly moved past it. I had to think action now. Not about Teddy. Not about anything.

The yakuza were ready, however. One of the men drew a knife. He rolled towards me quickly, angrily, ready to silence me once and for all. I could see the look on his face – *She got lucky, but she's not going to get out of here without coming with us.* I managed to slide into a shadow and elude him. He went crashing into a wall. The knife slipped from his grasp, dropping almost at my feet. I quickly grabbed it and shoved it into my pocket.

Another man careened towards me. There was someone at my back. I swirled and kicked. I managed to land a blow on someone's shoulder. One of them hit me on my side, but I managed not to fall. *Concentrate,* I told myself. *You're doing this. You're smarter than them!*

I could only see the task at hand. I knew that I had to employ the method Hiro and I had spoken about – using the shadows to dance in and out of. Using them to pit one of the attackers against the other. The man I'd hit first struggled to get up. Another rushed towards me. They were all ready in case one fell. I could tell they were all thinking, *This is ridiculous. This girl is small. She is no match.*

When the man rushing towards me was inches away, I found the shadow I needed. I quickly moved to the side. But not quickly enough. The guy moved, too, and rammed right into me. The second one lunged at me from the side. I gasped and nearly bit my tongue off. The two of them sandwiched me together, pulling and scraping and kicking and trying to tie me up in a knot. The Whisper screeched desperately out of my hand, sliding across the room with an angry wail.

One of the men took hold of me strongly while the other raced for the katana. He held me by my shoulders and tried to pick me up to flip me. I held his waist. We struggled in a strange dance for a few minutes. His hands dug into my skin. His knees beat relentlessly into my torso. I could see the others rushing towards me as well, hoping to form a pileup with Heaven in the middle.

"We don't want to hurt you," the guy whispered to me sinisterly. "We just want to talk to you. If you just let go peacefully, no one will get hurt."

Something in his voice told me not to believe him. I choked and gasped for air. *Is this it? Where is Hiro?* The man grunted and writhed and lifted me up. I saw, from above, my feet dangling in the air. I tried to pummel his chest. I did not want to be flipped – if I was, I would be knocked out for sure. I couldn't imagine the impact of him throwing me on the concrete. His arms around me felt like steel girders. He wrenched at my waist and squeezed. It felt like all my organs were being crushed. I desperately tried to kick and claw at him, using all of my body parts, but they were like feathers hitting him. He didn't even flinch. Instead he continued to squeeze me, holding my arm back from its socket, almost ready to break it, trying to lift me farther off the ground so he could throw me over to the other side of the room.

I could not be flipped. I could possibly pass out and then they would throw me into the car and take me where I needed to go. Or worse, they could kill me. What did they care? Yes, they needed Teddy and me to get married, but these men were ruthless.

I could no longer breathe. The other men came up to my side and began hitting me from all angles. I tried to bury my face in the man's chest. The pain was so extreme that some sort of survival mechanism kicked in – I actually began to feel nothing. In that moment I found myself drifting off, almost, losing consciousness. I looked around the room, ready to accept my fate. A strange calmness washed over me. And in that moment, a miraculous thing happened.

I saw Ohiko.

I saw him standing at the corner of the garage, his arms crossed against his chest. A strange light surrounded him, illuminating just his body, coming from some ethereal outside source. He held a sword like the Whisper at his side. He stared right at me, with a benevolent, relaxed look.

"Ohiko!" I screamed. I don't know if I actually screamed it out loud or not.

Ohiko stared at me and held the sword up in my direction. He stared at me for a very long time, silent. But above the din of the angry men pulling the life from me, I heard him speak. "Heaven," he said calmly. "You must help yourself."

"What do you mean?" I screamed.

"You have all the strength inside you to help yourself," Ohiko said calmly. "I will be watching. I know you can."

I looked for him in the next moment and couldn't see him. Where had he gone? I felt like I'd lost him once again.

I was jerked back to consciousness and drowning in pain. But then suddenly the wind shifted. It was like a golden light had descended upon me. My arms and legs began to move. My knees began to connect. Even my head became a weapon. I butted the guy's chest and used my fingers to drill into his solar plexus. He backed up in pain. I found my window. I managed to wrench myself free, then grabbed him around his middle and flipped him myself. It was as excruciating and terrible as when I'd flipped the other guy, but I managed to send him crashing to his back. Dust rose from the garage floor. A terrible rattling shook the rafters. The others backed away in surprise.

Ohiko said I had to help myself. That I had the strength inside me. I glared at the shadows and suddenly it all became clear. The swiftness, the lightness. I was focused. The next man ran towards me, even angrier than before. I found the shadow and this time conquered it. I slid in quickly, stealthily, and the man crashed into the wall. The next one raced towards me, yelling. I positioned myself near the man who'd just hit the wall and the second attacker changed direction. At the last second I found the shadow again. The second guy sprawled into the first. They both landed spread-eagled in a massive pile on the floor. I could hear gasping and wheezing from one of them – he must have had the wind knocked out of him.

I couldn't believe it. It was working. My plan was *working*.

The next man – I realised it the same guy who'd led us in – had found the Whisper at the other end of the room. He advanced towards me, waving it around dangerously. I dodged and weaved, trying to find the proper shadow. I moved around the room quickly – perhaps I would tire him out a little. Out of the corner of my eye I saw one of the other guys rushing up from behind. Ski mask loomed before me. I desperately searched for a shadow and found one. I held my breath and for a moment stood very still. The two men ran for me at once, ski mask with the Whisper blazing and the other guy with his meaty arms outstretched, ready to cut off my circulation. I clenched my jaw and at the last possible moment ducked, rolled, and disappeared into the shadow. For one slim second, I was invisible.

Crash. Body hit body in a thunderous clash of bone meeting bone, muscle smashing up against muscle. I could hear the strange conk of two heads knocking against each other. Like two dominoes, they fell down, one on top of the other. I stood in my shadowy corner and gaped.

I saw the glint of my katana in ski mask's hands. He still clutched it, even having fallen. I quickly dashed over to him and stood on his hand and moved my foot around, as if I was stamping out a cigarette. I could feel the bones in his fingers. It worked. He wailed in pain and released his grasp. I grabbed the Whisper and went back to my shadowy corner.

The other guy, who had fallen on top of ski mask, struggled to get up quickly. He got to his knees and saw me, flaring his nostrils like a bull. I slid out of my shadow and managed to give him a quick cut to his side. He screamed and collapsed back down. I knew that if I hadn't found my shadow, I could have been at the bottom of that pile. Or worse. I scanned the wreckage in the garage. The two guys who had run into the wall were groaning and getting to their feet.

Suddenly I heard a noise at the end of the garage. The rattling was back. All at once I saw a flood of lights from the street and the garage door was open. Hiro's silhouette was backlit by the yellow streetlights. He stood in the ready position. His arms flexed. He saw me and nodded. I knew not to say anything. The attackers were so dazed, many of them didn't even look in the direction of the door as Hiro walked in. The two that I hadn't hurt yet rushed towards Hiro. "Get out of here!" they rumbled.

I wanted to run to Hiro and throw my arms around him. I

wanted to kiss him just as passionately as I had in my dream and bury my head in his chest. But we had a job to do. I left him to his. I held up my sword and tended to mine.

Hiro quickly gave one a blow to the shoulder and the next a kick in the face. He spun and moved economically, beautifully. I knew we should move into our fighting plans that we'd devised the other day. I would elude them by bobbing into the shadows; Hiro, the stronger fighter, would take them to the ground with one of his powerful kicks.

I rushed over to the space in the wall to find the second hidden katana. With a glance in Hiro's direction, I caught his eye. He saw the glint of the metal; I threw it over to him. It arced gracefully in the sky and fell neatly into Hiro's hands.

Everyone was back on their feet now. Hiro twirled and spun. The attackers were confused about who to go after. Hiro and I stood close together, saying nothing, simply and silently trying to fight them down. I twirled around and around, ducking, rolling, stealthily forcing the attackers closer and closer to the shadows. Hiro followed. Eventually, when they would take a swing at me, I would collapse into the shadow and Hiro would slice them on the shoulder, leg, arm with the katana.

I thought of nothing else except where my attackers would try to strike me. It was like finally getting into the swing of swimming – I became efficient, focused, effortless. I knew the battleground and I began to understand the men who were try-ing to attack us. They were street fighters – brutal, dirty. They just wanted to get us in a body hold and then bring us down. They were slow and often swung for our faces. It just took some strategically placed ducks to send them off balance. One of the men swung at me. I crouched. His whole power settled into the swing; when it didn't connect, he became confused. And in that second of confusion, Hiro pounced.

Hiro and I continued to work together, spinning and ducking and kicking like clockwork. I didn't execute too many strategic fighting movements unless it was absolutely necessary to ward them off – my skills were still clumsy and a little slow. But what I lacked in technique I made up in stealth. Once I got the hang of it, it was incredible. I became a mere wisp of the shadows. Half the time the guys were swinging at thin air so far from where I was that it felt like I truly had become invisible, a shape shifter. Hiro managed to fell six of them. They all sat on the ground, stunned, swearing to themselves in Japanese. One phrase was repeated over and over: *Why didn't we bring a gun?*

Because, I thought. *You didn't think the little Kogo girl could fight.*

The seventh guy had become so tired that we didn't even have to do the shadow trick with him. Hiro just managed to catch him clumsily off guard and sent a blinding side kick to his jaw. The man ricocheted backwards, his body forming a perfect arc in the air. He landed with a horrendous thud on the garage floor. I could hear the crack of bone. He also landed on one of the guys' legs. There was screaming, confusion.

Hiro grabbed my hand and pulled me to the front of the garage, where the door was. I stared back at the men, all lying on the ground, groaning. The car with the door open still sat there, motionless. It would not be taking me anywhere tonight.

I couldn't believe it. We'd actually pulled it off.

"Come on," Hiro said in a whisper. "Let's go before they get up."

But for a moment I was transfixed. I had seen Ohiko. In the flesh. It had definitely been him, standing there, staring at me, with his sword, in the corner. Could it have been an illusion? A trick of the brain when I was losing oxygen? Or was he real? Could he really have found me when I most needed him?

He'd said he'd be watching me.

I stared at that corner, looking for a trick of the light. But it looked like the rest of the garage. Nothing unusual. Dust rose up from the floor and danced around. One of the Yukemura men let out a very large groan. The smell of blood and sweat filled the air.

"Come on," Hiro said through his teeth. He grabbed my wrist. I whipped my head around and saw two of the men delicately standing. Were they coming for more? We started to run, our shoes clattering against the pavement. I looked back, expecting them to follow. But they didn't. The two that stood just remained there, motionless, shaking their heads. They almost looked at us with a sense of respect. I felt transcendent. I had become a vapour.

"I have to say, Heaven, I was amazed that you had them in the position you did once I managed to get inside," Hiro said as we rushed away. "You had four of them down. And in pain!"

"I used the shadow trick," I said excitedly.

"I know – over and over again!" He beamed at me. "It was incredible!"

"It was definitely the Yukemuras," I said breathlessly. "They wanted to complete the wedding."

We ran down the empty sidewalks of lower L.A. Hiro didn't break stride. I decided not to explain anything about seeing Ohiko. I wanted it to be my own private memory. "They mean business."

"They do," Hiro said. "I'm glad you and Karen are safe."

"Did the exchange go okay? Were there any guys out front that you had to deal with guarding the garage?"

"There was one guy, but I freaked him out just by hitting him. I didn't even hit him hard, really. He ran off." I could see, even while running, a look of concern cross his face. "I hope everything's okay with the car and Karen. I left it pretty far away – it's about ten blocks still. I didn't think anyone would follow us when we left. I didn't see anyone, and I drove pretty slow, keeping a lookout."

"Is Karen okay?"

"She seems to be," Hiro said. "She seems tired and confused, really. She didn't say much. She was very understanding about the fact that I had to go back for you. Getting that door open was tough." He stared at his hands. "I sliced my finger open."

"I guess they didn't want anyone to get in," I said. "And—" I started to say something else, but I stopped. I saw the car parked alone on a small side street. It was ensconced in darkness. From our vantage point, we couldn't see if anyone was inside.

"Is she there?" I whispered. My heart began to race. Were other Yukemuras staked out here?

But then we saw the outline of a dark ponytail and Karen's profile. "Karen!" Hiro called. It looked like she was fine. Hiro turned to me with a gracious look in his eyes. All of a sudden he threw his arms around me. I was surrounded by Hiro's body, and it felt so good. Just as warm as in my dream. "Thank you," he said. "Thank you so much."

"Thank *you*," I whispered against his shoulder. At that moment I wanted to tell him everything. That I'd been near death before he came in. That Ohiko had inspired me – enlightened me, maybe. Given me superhuman strength. I don't know. That I had fallen so hard for him. That I would do anything for him. But instead I just wrapped my arms around him and sighed.

We rushed into the car. Karen was sitting in the front seat, and she immediately sat up and burst into tears. "You guys are okay!" she wailed. She stretched her arms out to hug Hiro and then pulled me in from the backseat with her other arm. Her body shook with sobs. I reached over and patted her shoulder, and she shot me a grateful look through a veil of tears. With Karen's arms still wrapped around us, Hiro quickly started the car and drove us away. I hugged Karen back and felt a pang of horrible guilt. It must have been a nightmare for Karen over the last couple of days. And again, all because of me.

When Hiro braked for a light, he and Karen embraced passionately. Karen kissed him on the ear, tears still washing down her face. "I'm so glad you're okay," she said over and over again.

"Yeah, Heaven had them all down for the count by the time I got there," Hiro said. We both laughed. Karen looked at us with wide eyes, then went back to hugging Hiro. Things would be different now. Karen would need to know something. Details about my life, sketchy as they might be. I would have

THE BOOK OF THE SHADOW

to tell her. I couldn't expect her to be kidnapped and not ask questions. I couldn't expect her to sit in the car, waiting, without wondering what the deal was. She had probably seen all sorts of things in the presence of the Yukemuras. Even if they'd spoken in Japanese around her, she still must have some memories burned into the innermost part of her brain.

I bit my lip, thinking about revealing my story to Karen. To anyone. What would happen. And what would happen to me, anyway? Was this over, done for? I didn't know.

I directed my eyes to the sky. Somewhere off in Hollywood searchlights danced around, announcing something wonderful, perhaps a film premiere. But I had been given something more wonderful right here with my amazing, angelic sighting of Ohiko. What could that have been? *Thank you,* I thought. *Thank you, Ohiko. Wherever you are.*

Hiro and Karen continued to embrace. I leaned back against my seat, exhausted. At a stoplight I saw them kiss. Desperately. As they should. My heart pounded and my brain swam with my breakthrough of becoming invisible. But in all, it felt a little bittersweet. Tinged with disappointment. The drama of the kidnapping had brought Karen and Hiro even closer together. I really was a vapour. In more ways than one.

16

Three days after the exchange, my body still ached from my attackers' blows. Strange images haunted me – images of being immersed in the one's body, kicked from all sides. But I made peace with them. After all, moments later I'd managed to hurt them more than they'd hurt me.

I was trying to lay low. It had been a quiet few days. Hiro and I had resumed practise at the dojo, at least for now. We figured the Yukemuras would be hesitant to try to kidnap me again so soon. They knew that we were a force to contend with. Still, I felt a little on edge. I knew that I had the strength to defend myself if I happened to meet Yoji Yukemura in a dark corner some night, but I didn't like the idea of it actually *happening*.

I sat at the dojo after practise, massaging my arms and legs. I could hear Karen's shouts to her class in the other room. Apparently the kidnappers hadn't treated her very well. She'd stayed for those three days in a small room of an office building, most of the time blindfolded. She couldn't remember where it was. There'd been only two men, she remembered, but they only spoke in Japanese. It had been a very confusing and stressful time. I was amazed that she'd resumed teaching so quickly. "She just wants to get past it," Hiro said. "She's pretty amazing that way."

Hiro came and sat next to me while I was giving my legs a rubdown. He put his hands on my shoulders and massaged them. I felt the usual tingles. They weren't even surprising anymore. "What have you told Karen about all of this?" I asked him.

"Not much," he said. "I told her the basics – that you were arranged to marry someone from Japan, someone in a very prestigious family, but that you had refused, so they decided they would kidnap you. Karen didn't ask any questions. I think she's too mentally exhausted or overwhelmed right now to ask."

"Well, she must think that my family is awfully weird if people are going around kidnapping brides-to-be," I said, laughing despite the situation. It was so awful, it was almost funny. But sad, too. It was the sort of laugh that could easily turn into a cry.

"She may want to know things later on, though," Hiro said. "We'll have to figure out what to tell her."

I looked at him. "Thank you so much," I said. "For everything. For putting up with me. For keeping my situation a secret. For allowing Teddy to beat you up. For . . . everything."

"It's nothing," Hiro said. "It's my obligation. And I didn't tell you the other day – you have mastered a skill that some never master in their lives. You have learned to use your body to become a shadow. You have made the mind-body connection.

It's amazing. And you learned it so quickly. I am completely floored by your talent, Heaven."

I ducked my head. "I can't even explain how it came along," I said. "It just . . . happened."

"That's just it," Hiro said. "This is a skill that you can practise and practise and practise and still maybe not get. You might *feel* like you've got it, but in fact you haven't. I think you learned that when one of the yakuza kobun saw you on the street."

I nodded.

"You have amazing natural talent. Honestly. I didn't know how it would go in the beginning. I've told you that. And we haven't been as close as usual since you moved out. I know you've had to make some hard transitions, some difficult decisions. But Heaven, I am honoured to be your sensei. I think eventually your talent will outrank mine. And then you will have to be my teacher."

I blushed.

Hiro went on. "I think, actually, that is why you thought you achieved your mission so quickly. Because your natural talent and sense for things is so strong that you felt that you really had got there. But you must learn, Heaven, that your missions are to be accomplished when they're really ready to be accomplished. You cannot force them. They must find you."

I shifted in my seat. "You know, when I talked to Teddy before the exchange, he told me the kidnapping was just so he could marry me. Do you think that's true? When I was in there with them, alone, that's what they told me. And I recognised a few of them as members of the yakuza. Some of them were at our wedding."

"It sounds like that could have been it," Hiro said.

"But I have a theory . . . What if they just wanted to kill me and be done with it?" I said. "Make up a fake marriage certifi-cate. Have me married, have Teddy get the company, do what-ever it is they intend to do, and I'm dead, so I can't protest." Shivers went up my back just thinking about it. "Do you think that's possible?"

"It could be," Hiro said. "You still have to be very careful. I'm sure you're still going to be followed. We need to figure out some of the big questions, though. And figure out how to stop the yakuza."

"I really think it's the Yukemuras who are behind all of this," I said. "Everything. And maybe even the attack at the wedding. Some of those guys in there looked so familiar, like the same guys who attacked me on the street. But why would they be after *me*? And Ohiko? And . . . everyone?" I sighed. The world definitely wasn't safe. "Although," I said, "there is one thing: At least I know that it's not my father who is trying to end my life." I thought about my father for a moment. In all of the strangeness of the last few days I hadn't thought of him much. I'd thought more about Ohiko, the strange apparition who had helped me escape marriage or pain or . . . worse. I thought again of what my father had told me at our last meet-ing – that Ohiko had betrayed our family. Now I realised that he must have believed Ohiko was working for a rival gang. But I knew in my heart, just as I'd been sure from the minute he told me this, that it couldn't be true. Ohiko would never be part of the yakuza, not even to please my father. Which meant someone had lied to my father. Who? The Yukemuras? What could they possibly gain?

I wondered if my father had recovered. Or if he was still in the same state. My poor father. What was happening to him right now?

I thought about Teddy and how he'd helped us. If it hadn't been for Teddy, things would be incredibly different now. I shuddered to think how. But that didn't make sense either. If, say, Teddy had lied to us, and we'd met at another location, one we hadn't planned on. If, then, the attackers had managed to knock me out and Hiro hadn't made it back to help me. Then I would have married Teddy. Wasn't that what Teddy wanted? Or didn't he? Then what had he been talking about on the bus?

"It's pretty amazing that Teddy actually gave us the right information," I said to Hiro.

Hiro nodded. "I'd meant to talk to you about that, too. What do you think made him do such a thing?"

I shook my head. "I have no idea. Honestly. The more I think about it, the stranger it seems. Why would he allow us to escape?"

I began to get angry again, the same kind of anger I'd felt a few times before. I had to get answers. Teddy had steered me in the right direction once before; was it possible he could help me again?

"I think I'm going to try and reach him again," I said to Hiro. "To find out about his family's motives."

To my surprise, Hiro didn't tell me not to. He just looked up at the ceiling, his eyes closed. Karen's shouts drifted in from the other room. "Do what you have to do," he said. It almost seemed like he was beginning to trust my instincts over his own.

I rushed to my bag to find the last remaining disposable cell phone. I found Teddy's number as well. It was definitely the Yukemuras who'd planned the kidnapping. They'd all but admitted it freely. But what else were they behind? Would Teddy help me? What if he really was an ally? What if he was just a pawn in this strange game, like me?

Punching in the number, I thought of something else. *Isn't Teddy in big trouble with the Colombians?* Surely his father wouldn't help him now that something had gone wrong with kidnapping me. Why? I shakily punched in the last two digits. The phone waited a few seconds, then started ringing. And ringing. And ringing.

Finally an automated voice picked up. "We're sorry. The number you are trying to call has been disconnected. There is no further information on this number. Thank you." Then the angry buzzing of the dial tone.

I stared at the phone. Somehow I just knew.

Teddy was gone.

I guess it's night. I'm totally stuck here. No outside contact. No Ojo. Don't know where he is. No television. No way out. I've gone through the scenarios in my head. Did I do the right thing? I don't know.

I can hear the sound of a leaky faucet. I lie here in the darkness of day or night – I don't know what time it is. I stare and can't do anything really except deal with my thoughts and what I've done wrong.

I wish I could tell her. Get an e-mail out to her and tell her something. A mental message. Wish I could tell her something. Somehow. The dripping sink just won't stop. I told the truth. Does she realise what I went through? After? The mental anguish, even before? I knew what would happen. I knew they'd find out. It wasn't a stealth operation. People know. But Heaven's a smart girl. She knew about the yakuza. She knew about my life. She might be able to figure it out. Day, night, whatever it is right now, she's there, somewhere, hopefully alive, hopefully free. If she weren't, I guess I'd be married to her now, is that right? Is that really what they were going to do? I don't even know. I'd be married to her if I had lied. So why didn't I?

But I didn't lie, Heaven. I didn't lie to you. Why? I've been wrestling with that question here in the dark. Wrestling about you. I told you because . . . I told you because . . . something. I told you, I think, Heaven, Heaven Kogo, because I think . . . maybe . . . I love you.

Teddy

Coming soon . . .

sαmurαi girl The Book of the Pearl

I'm more alone now than I've ever been.

But at the same time, I'm more free. My best friend says she can show me a new world. And I am ready to get out of this one.

At night, L.A. turns into a theme park. Heroes, thugs, party girls – they all get together and dance. No one should trust the people they meet at night.

I shouldn't take changes right now. But I must . . .

I am Samurai Girl.

Turn the page for the first chapter . . .

Tokyo Daily News

Authorities remain silent about the ongoing investigation of the death of Ohiko Kogo, son of business scion Konishi Kogo (of Kogo Industries fame). Details have been slow to surface in the mysterious death, which took place at the Los Angeles wedding of Kogo's adopted daughter, Heaven, to Takeda "Teddy" Yukemura, son of the prominent Yukemura family. Sources have leaked numerous contradictory details to the press, but the following facts have been verified: an intruder (some say a ninja) invaded the wedding, killing Ohiko Kogo after a violent sword fight witnessed by dozens of guests. Heaven Kogo fled the scene, and it is unclear whether she remains in the United States or has returned to Japan. Several weeks ago Konishi Kogo was flown back to Tokyo in a coma after another reputed ninja attack. Authorities once again refused to comment on rumours that Heaven Kogo may have been involved in the second attack. Konishi Kogo remains in a coma at an undisclosed location. His wife, Mieko, has refused repeated requests for an interview. Heaven Kogo, of course, first caught the nation's attention in 1984 at the age of six months as the sole survivor of Japan Airlines flight 999, which crashed en route from Tokyo to Los Angeles. When no family members surfaced to claim the child, Konishi and Mieko Kogo stepped forward to adopt her . . .

1

"Are you sure you know where you're going?" I asked.

"Trust me." Cheryl laughed and tugged at her microscopic denim skirt, which managed to cover even less of her after she pulled it down. I wrapped my sweatshirt around me and scanned the area. We'd hopped off the bus near Second and Alameda – *not* a part of town I'd ever been in. Of course, I'd only been in L.A. for a couple of months, but something told me only Cheryl, my insane roommate, would think she could find a good time in this neighbourhood. Still, a ripple of excitement passed through me. It felt good to be out of the house.

"What are those tents?" I asked, pointing to an empty lot crammed full of oddly constructed shacks. Dark figures lurked over a burning trash can, warming themselves against the chilly California night.

"Those are homeless people, Heaven. Don't you have

those in Japan?"

"Of – of course," I stuttered, trying to mask my surprise. "Just not – exactly like that." I'd actually never seen a homeless person until I got to the States. I'd grown up in teeming, frenetic Tokyo, but my father's compound was like an oasis in that city. Servants, chauffeured cars, unlimited credit cards, cooks, a gym, a pool – you name it, we had it.

It's a simple story, really, if a little unusual. Baby falls out of a burning plane. Baby named "Heaven" by witty journalist, becomes national celebrity, Japan's "good-luck girl." Baby adopted by Konishi Kogo, head of Kogo Industries and the source of all that wealth I mentioned. Luck holds. Baby grows into Girl. Girl loves father. Girl grows up. Father tells Girl she has to marry Teddy Yukemura, slimy son of business rival. Girl obeys, travels to Los Angeles for hugely elaborate wedding. Wedding crashed by evil ninja. Ninja kills Girl's brother and only ally, Ohiko. Girl flees scene. Luck runs out.

"I think it's this way." Cheryl turned onto a smaller street that was totally devoid of people. I instinctively went into alert mode, casting my senses out like feelers – sort of the same way Spider-Man unfurls his spider goo. (I had developed a huge crush on Tobey Maguire after Cheryl downloaded that movie. Dreamy. Did I mention I'm a total movie-phile?) I didn't sense anything out of the ordinary, but I was still tempted to use some of the stealth techniques I'd learned just to make sure we got to wherever we were going.

I resisted, thinking Cheryl might find it odd if her roomie suddenly began slipping in and out of existence like a ghost. It was just a trick of the eye and mind, really, but it could still be freaky.

Oh – there's one other thing I didn't mention. After Girl went on the lam? Girl became Samurai Girl. Well, Samurai Girl in training. But still.

"Are you sure you know where you're going?" I grabbed Cheryl's jacket and stopped her in her tracks. "There's nothing that even remotely resembles a nightclub here."

"Hehh-vuuuuhn . . . ," Cheryl moaned, rolling her eyes. "Trust me. We agreed that you need this. Remember? All you've been doing for the last week is lying around the house, polluting your mind with bad television and your body with Krispy Kremes."

"I have *not* eaten that many Krispy Kremes," I insisted, laughing. Maybe it was true that I had an unholy affection for the little fried lard puffs. Blame it on the strictly healthy Eastern diet I was raised on. But I wasn't a total addict . . . yet.

"Krispy Kremes aren't even the point. Ever since you and Hiro had that *thing,* which you *still* haven't explained to me, and you got fired from Life Bytes—"

"I did not get *fired*. I quit."

"Whatever. The point is you've been moping around like a sick puppy. You have to get back out there and live a little. Besides, you owe me for this month's rent. That *alone* should be enough to inspire you to hit the job market. And

a night at Vibe is going to put you back in action. Trust me."
Cheryl's stiletto boots tapped the pavement as she teetered
over to the corner and squinted up at the street sign. "Ooh!
Peabody. This is it. Let's go."

"I *am* inspired!" I argued as Cheryl skipped off, her
cropped blonde head (complete with bright pink streaks)
bobbing. "But why not just go somewhere on the Strip?"
Cheryl ignored me, and I tried to rekindle the feeling of
excitement at our big night out. I hated feeling like I
wasn't able to take care of myself, having to borrow
money (especially from someone like Cheryl, who didn't
have a lot of it) when I'd never had to worry about money
before. Never even had to consider it. But I was on my own
now, and I'd had to quit the first job I'd ever got (at an
Internet café) when my almost-husband's family, the
Yukemuras, decided they wanted to kidnap me. I was
pretty sure by now that the Yukemuras were out to destroy
the Kogos and were responsible for my brother's murder.
But there were still so many pieces to the puzzle. My
brother, who was also my best friend, was dead. My father
had been flown back to Japan in a coma, the victim of
another ninja attack. And Hiro, my trainer, the man who
saved me, was in love with another woman, Karen. And
she had ended up being kidnapped when she was mistaken for me. I was alone.

How very *Days of Our Lives,* right?

"Wait up!" I called as I caught up with Cheryl, who was

speeding towards the faint sound of a thumping bass.

"Okay, Heaven, just be cool," Cheryl whispered theatrically as we turned the corner and saw a bunch of people hanging around outside a nondescript storefront. "Take off that sweatshirt."

"It's freezing," I whined, pulling the sleeves down over my hands. "Besides, I'm not sure about this outfit you made me wear." Cheryl always managed to convince me to wear something I never would normally. Tonight it was a pair of low-slung jeans with a leather belt that sat on my hips and a flowing black top that slid off one shoulder. I'd refused to wear heels, instead choosing a pair of motorcycle boots from Cheryl's vast shoe collection.

I knew I had to be able to run. But more on that later.

"Give it here," Cheryl chirped, ignoring me. She opened her cavernous shoulder bag and held out her hand. I stripped off my sweatshirt and stood there awkwardly, feeling half naked and stupid. Cheryl looked at me critically.

"God, you are one lucky woman. Whatever kind of training you and Hiro do, it's working. Can you say 'Charlie's Angel'?"

"Shut up, dork," I said, blushing. I still wasn't used to getting compliments.

"Okay. Here's the deal," Cheryl said, suddenly all business. "Vibe is underground. That means they don't really have a licence to be here, and they only advertise by word of mouth. So we have to be very chill – plus we don't look like hip-hop regulars, so just play it cool. Do you have that ID I gave you?"

I fished in the back pocket of my jeans and pulled out the fake ID Cheryl had made for me. Just having it made me feel instantly cooler, like a "normal" teenager. I suppressed a giggle as I looked at it. There was nothing Cheryl couldn't do. A few weeks before, she'd dragged me into the bathroom and done my makeup, then taken me to a photo booth in a nearby mall for pictures. And now there I was, grinning out from the plastic card, complete with an assumed name – Heaven Johnson. I wasn't sure of my ethnic background, since I was adopted, but it was pretty certain that I was half Caucasian. And with the ID, I'd aged from nineteen to twenty-three overnight – presto! Every inch the California girl.

"All right, let's go," Cheryl said, giving me a last once-over. You would have thought we were about to go into battle. That was one of the things I loved about Cheryl – she took having a good time *seriously*.

The bouncer was sitting on a stool, talking to a few guys in baggy jeans and do-rags. He looked us up and down, then waved us in without another glance. "Have a good time, ladies," he said. I heard one of the guys whistle before the heavy iron door closed behind us. I glanced back, and another guy grinned at me, displaying a row of gold teeth. I looked away quickly and shivered. I hoped Cheryl knew what she was getting us into . . .